Edward C Caswell

OLD NEW ORLEANS

STRIFE

The Seventies

By EDWARD LAROCQUE TINKER

LAFCADIO HEARN'S AMERICAN DAYS (1924)

TOUCOUTOU (1928)

(In collaboration with Frances Tinker)

OLD NEW ORLEANS (1931)
- Widows Only (The Sixties)
- Strife (The Seventies)
- Closed Shutters (The Eighties)
- Mardi Gras Masks (The Nineties)

OLD NEW ORLEANS

STRIFE

The Seventies

BY

FRANCES TINKER

AND

EDWARD LAROCQUE TINKER

FRONTISPIECE BY JOSEPH PENNELL

DECORATIONS BY EDWARD C. CASWELL

D. APPLETON AND COMPANY
NEW YORK   LONDON   MCMXXXI

To

ELIZABETH ROBINS PENNELL

STRIFE

The Seventies

STRIFE

The Seventies

NOT a window blind had been open the whole day long in all New Orleans, for the mid-June Sunday was so stifling that the slats were tilted only a trifle. As the afternoon passed, the impassive, sealed façades of the fashionable houses of the Vieux Carré belied the hectic bustle going on in the twilight of their huge high-ceilinged rooms.

"White chillun" were being dressed in starched frilly clothes by their mammies, and pretty Creole mothers hurried around undoing *papillotes,* brushing curls into corkscrews of mechanical precision and giving a dab of gluey quince seed to young hopefuls' obdurate cowlicks.

[3]

A little girl of twelve with a wreath of pale tea roses on her blonde curls came out on a gallery in Esplanade Avenue. As she stood between the tall Greek columns, in her filmy white organdy dress, she seemed as small and fragile as a silver night-moth.

"Wait, Elodie, we can't go till yo' Maw an Paw come," called a rich negro voice from the door as Catiche appeared, her white apron almost entirely hidden by a huge basket, full of roses, which she carried on her arm. Her dress of brown-figured indienne toned in pleasantly with her thin, dusky face and her jauntily tied *tignon* of brilliant reds and yellows made her look like some barbaric flower of the tropics.

"Can't we go over to the Duplantiers' and wait there?" urged Elodie. "Mother's nervous and cross this evening and she's sure to be late."

Catiche glanced at the little girl furtively. "You mus'n' talk dat away, yo' Maw ain' cross, she sick."

"Yes, but she can't be sick all the time and she's always nervous and cross."

Her nurse started to answer her just as Monsieur and Madame Labatut reached the porch and, closing the front door carefully, they all went down the steps and across the street. The one-mule tram car rattled by on the neutral ground and the noise of laughing, chattering children drowned any chance remark until they reached the iron gate that opened on the side garden of the Duplantiers' house, almost directly opposite their own.

Gay borders of lavender, pink and purple larkspur lined the walk to the door and a screen of crêpe-myrtle hid the

back of the house. Their crinkly rosy
blossoms looked like showers of confetti;
a pink nimbus floating around the naked
branches. Stiletto-leaved bamboos and
two magnolia trees starred with blanched
blossoms, gave the yard a sense of privacy
and the faint perfume of many flowers
floated everywhere.

Madame Duplantier was waiting for
them on the gallery. As she hurried forward to kiss the slightly faded yet still
pretty face of her neighbor from across
the street, she said gaily, "Oh! my dear
Marilisse! What trouble I have had with
the hair of Doudouce. It was as stubborn
and straight as the tail of a little mule."
To Monsieur she gave her hand and he
raised it to his lips.

"With you it is only the hair of Doudouce that is stubborn, but with me it was
everything — Elodie, Catiche, Jacques.

[6]

They worried me so I have a sick head-
ache. I am always the one to suffer,"
answered Marilisse, her voice taking on
the pettish edge characteristic of the
anaemic woman who is perennially tired
and querulous.

Quick steps sounded in the hall. "Oh!
it's Doudouce," cried Elodie excitedly as
a little girl came running out, calling,
*"Maman, maman, regardez donc comme
je suis belle!"* Stopping in front of her
mother and holding out her skirts she
pirouetted so fast her long curls swung
out in a black circle around her head.

"Prenez garde, ma petite, you will lose
your crown and besides do you not see
Monsieur and Madame Labatut?"

After Doudouce had made her little
reverence, they loitered in the cool shady
garden until, with much fussing and fum-
ing, Monsieur Duplantier joined them

[7]

and they all started up Esplanade Avenue
towards the old St. Louis Cathedral on
Jackson Square. Doudouce's nurse had
a large basket of roses too, and the parti-
colored *tignons* and smiling black faces
were a gay queue to the little procession.

Bows and smiles were being constantly
interchanged with the other groups of
people coming from the side streets that
swelled the crowd going to the *Fête Dieu.*
The eyes of the men quickly passed over
Marilisse's frail prettiness and lingered
on Artémise Duplantier's extraordinary
beauty, nor was this surprising for she had
that indefinable attraction which has cap-
tivated men since the days of Helen of
Troy—and before.

Unusually tall for a Creole, her carriage was perfect, and the effortless ease
with which she moved could only be compared with the flowing motion of a tigress.

[8]

She radiated vitality and perfect physical
health—not the blatant kind of the blowsy
dairy maid but the unconscious, unques-
tioned normality of the perfect animal.
This was the cause of many a lifted eye-
brow among her sex, since it was a day
when delicate health and fainting were
still the marks of gentility.

"See, Popo," whispered Marilisse as
they walked along, "all these ladies look
with envy on Arté's gowns and that lovely
chapeau bergère. It must have come
from Madame Olympe's, for no one else
imports those ravishing solferino azaleas."

"It did all right; she pretends not to
care about clothes, but she thinks of nothing else," answered Duplantier angrily.
"If you ladies would stop throwing money
away on laces and furbelows, and," he continued guardedly, "buy guns for the
League, we'd stand a better chance of

making this a white man's country again."

"Please, Popo," complained Marilisse, her thin-lipped mouth drooping at the corners, "don't be so grumpy and sour. You haven't said a pleasant word all the way."

In a few moments they came to the square in the center of which the bronze statue of Andrew Jackson, hat in hand, astride his perennially prancing horse, surveyed with cold eyes the shell walks with their bordering shrubs, acacia trees and tousle-headed palms, all enclosed in a high black iron fence. On each of the four sides was a large massive gate topped with ornamental gas lanterns, while across Chartres Street the quaint old cathedral pointed its triple steeples to Heaven.

The two mothers, counseling the nurses to find Father Ambrose and turn the little rose-crowned girls and the baskets of flowers over to him, watched them disappear into the cool, dark interior of the candle-lighted cathedral, which, together with the twin Spanish buildings on each side, was the peak of the architectural charm of the city. Indeed these archaic edifices were its very sentimental center, for before their gray walls had been enacted every historical event of any importance that had occurred in New Orleans; the colorful pageant of the ceding of this great territory of Louisiana by France to Spain, its return to France and its almost immediate sale to the United States.

The Labatuts and Duplantiers made their way against the surging crowd coming from every direction, and crossed the street to the shade under the broad gallery with its iron railings of intertwined

[11]

initials and floriated curlycues. When
the dominating Baroness Pontalba built
these brick apartments an "islet" long and
their replica on the other side of the
square, they immediately became the
homes of the élite, and now aristocratic
ladies in colorful frills, with their large
hats drooping under their burden of brilliant artificial flowers, made lovely pictures against its red façade and trans-
formed the two galleries into long flanking
parterres in a hanging garden of gay,
riotous beauty.

They entered a high narrow door and
started up the steep, twisting stair with
its hand-rail of Santo Domingo ma-
hogany.

"Jacques," asked Popo mysteriously,
his voice sullen and faultfinding, "have
you joined the White League?"

Arté glanced back with uneasiness.

"No. I'm a Frenchman. I have no business with local politics."

"You have no business with local politics?" railed Popo, his face red with sudden anger. "You're making your living here. Can you call yourself a decent white man if you don't raise a finger to stop that mob of black *macaques* and disreputable carpet-baggers from robbing the state? Every time I see that nigger ape, Caius César Antoine, who used to black my boots on a river steamboat, strutting 'round in a top hat and green gloves, and realize he's the Lieutenant-Governor of Louisiana, I want to go out and lynch every damn one of them."

"Ssh!" cautioned Arté, "stop talking politics, I get nothing else every day."

They entered a large high room, cool and dusky. The furniture, swathed in summer covers, had a spectral look in the

[13]

dim light from the French open window
onto the gallery.

Through it came Professor Colegnon,
mopping his head. The voluminous tails
of his black alpaca frock coat fluttered
as he hurried across the mattinged floor.

"Ah! I am so happy to see you all," he
said as he greeted them. "I do not have
to ask that you are well. And my little
pupils, are they in the *Fête Dieu?*"

"Oh, yes, Professor, that is why we are
in such good time."

He hurried them across the floor and
out into the sunshine where short, fat
Madame Colegnon had saved chairs for
them near the iron railing. From there
they could look down upon the restless
activity of the waiting crowd and beyond
to the levee, piled high with bales and
hogsheads. Along its edge were moored
river steamboats and sailing ships, their

twin funnels belching black smoke and
their masts and rigging making lacy an-
gular patterns against the sky.

Despite Arté's wishes Popo continued
his tirade, and her scowls and frowns de-
terred him not at all. When some one
mentioned Kellogg, he suddenly seemed
to have lost all control of his anger, which
flamed up fanatically.

"Yes, it's an outrage for that offscour-
ing of the North to be our Governor.
What does he know of Louisiana? He
came here less than ten years ago, dead
broke, without a dollar to his name, but
now he's rich."

Professor Colegnon was disturbed at
the unwise outburst, and he saw that many
of his other guests felt the same way, so
without taking issue he tried to minimize
its importance and give the conversation
a jocular twist. "I read a funny little

rhyme about him some time ago," he said laughingly. "It was in the *Carillon,* I think, and went something like,

> *"The other day in a swampy bog,*
>   *A serpent bit William Pitt Kellogg.*
> *Who was poisoned, do you say?*
> *The snake; it died that very day."*

Every one laughed.

A chord on the cathedral organ pealed forth and interest in Kellogg and his black and tan legislature was suspended for the *Fête Dieu.* As the doors were flung open the pent-up music filled Jackson Square and two red-coated beadles marched out. They were gold-trimmed and tasselled and their baldrics of purple silk bore round silver plates embossed with the arms of the Pope. With pompous step they advanced to the middle of the street and, as they fell in behind the

[16]

waiting military band, the procession started.

Then various Catholic organizations, the Society of St. Vincent de Paul and of St. Louis de Gonzague streamed out like a double line of black ants. A priest came next, carrying aloft a tall cross of gold. His accompanying acolytes, gay-hued as redbirds, held long, lighted candles and the little children—La Sainte Enfance—followed him as if he were a Pied Piper.

"Oh, here come the Enfants de Marie," called Arté excitedly as blue-sashed girls began to emerge from the dark maw of the cathedral. When their blue banner with its picture of the Virgin went by, the people crossed themselves.

Jacques Labatut watched it with the greatest interest. "After all," he said, turning to Professor Colegnon, "the Catholic church is marvellous. It has an impeccable instinct for stirring the emotions with pageantry. See how cleverly the red robes of those altar boys swinging censers tune in with the rest of the colors —like musical chords in a great sonata."

"There's no clever conscious art in that," the host replied, "no more than there is in that priest's deep, clear voice intoning the Litany—that's Faith, sincere Faith, and those high, sweet, bell-like responses of the choir boys—you can't call that art, can you?"

"Of course, the mind that evolved the idea of that contrast had an unerring feeling for effect."

"No, no, you're wrong. You Frenchmen are different from us Creoles. You've been reading too much Voltaire, and we still think it's a sin to look at such books. Religion should not be coldly

[18]

analyzed, it should be felt—here," the little professor thumped his thin bent chest. "What you are doing, is like listening to a well trained orchestra play a masterpiece, and wondering all the time how the trombonist oiled his slide, or the violinist tuned his fiddle."

Marilisse and Arté were sitting on the edges of their chairs—Doudouce and Elodie must come soon.

"Oh! quick—Jacques! Popo! here they are," they called excitedly, as ten little rose-crowned girls appeared. They carried light, wicker trays piled high with roses, which they scattered before the parish priest who bore aloft in both hands a richly chased Monstrance with its halo of golden rays. The crowd knelt with bowed heads at the approach of the Sacred Vessel.

"Santa Maria!" chanted a solemn voice,

as the procession made its way down
Chartres Street, whose overhanging galleries were packed with people.

"Ora pro nobis!" the multitude droned
in response.

"Santo Bartholoméo!"

"Ora pro nobis!"

"Santa Philoména!"

"Ora pro nobis!"

After the Host had passed the crowd
rose from their knees and Madame Colegnon began to babble about the children.
"The professor was so pleased to see that
Elodie and Doudouce were leading," she
said. "He is proud of his little pupils.
How exquisite their dresses were, and
how beautifully they behaved—not at all
like Odile's daughter who was right behind them. She shows the coarse strain of
an American father. Perhaps her mother
touched plenty money but she lowered

herself when she married that Monsieur
Fin-er-ran."

"Yes," interrupted Artémise, "they
even say he has become a Republican."

"What a disgrace," chorused the guests.

"He should be tarred and feathered,"
broke in Popo angrily.

"But, *mon ami,* after all," countered
Jacques Labatut in his calm, sensible
way, "isn't he as much entitled to his
opinions on politics as you are?"

"Please! please!" whispered Arté, as
Popo exploded in staccato French, wav-
ing both arms wildly as he talked.

No one could stop him and he vitu-
perated on against the Yankee scum and
dirty niggers and carpet-baggers and
Northern bayonets, much to every one's
embarrassment.

"There'll be a change soon, you'll see,"
he wound up excitedly as Marilisse and

Arté could stand it no longer and rose
to go, wearied irritation showing on their
faces. Madame Colegnon was particularly upset, and the miniature of her husband on her abundant bosom palpitated
with regret because they could not wait
to see the procession come back and have
some "collation."

As they started down the winding
stairs Marilisse was almost in tears. "Too
bad!" she said complainingly, "some one
always spoils a party. I'm not well
enough to stand the annoyance. It makes
me nervous." She caught her breath, "I
did so want to see whether Elodie had
fixed her wreath yet. It was just like her
father's hats, they always tilt a little."

Jacques unconsciously straightened his
panama and a fleeting look of annoyance
passed over his face.

Madame Duplantier was biting her full

lips and her cheeks flushed a deep red
under her rich, warm skin. Halfway
down she stopped suddenly. "Why don't
you and Jacques stay? There is no reason for your leaving just because Popo
has made the whole afternoon unbear-
able."

Her husband's heavy face was surly but
he said nothing.

"No," Marilisse answered hesitatingly
in her too sweet, whining voice. "Now
that we've started we might as well go
home. I can never enjoy anything after
I'm upset."

"Is there ever a time when you're not
upset?" asked Jacques petulantly.

"Pour l'amour de Dieu!" interrupted
Arté. "Can no one be pleasant? Popo's
bad enough without any help."

The streets were almost empty, for the
crowd had fallen back to the garden in

the rear of the cathedral where the procession had made its first stop. Artémise walked rapidly ahead but Jacques caught up with her at the corner just as the parish priest, carrying the Host, had ascended the steps to the *reposoir* which was draped with gold-encrusted red velvet. Innumerable candles flickered on each side and their yellow flames were reflected in the glittering Monstrance which the father held high above his head. The crowd kneeled and the Sacred Vessel was moved in the sign of the cross. When the blessing was over Arté and Jacques looked around for their companions but they were nowhere to be seen, so they took the nearest way home.

"I'm sorry I showed my irritation but Popo's constant tirades and Marilisse's faultfinding are just too much when they come together."

[24]

"I understand, Jacques, no one knows better than I how many times we've held our tempers but it's all we can do. I've grown to depend on you." She touched his arm. "You mustn't fail me. That would be too much to bear."

"I never will again," he murmured. "My life isn't as hard as yours, although at times it's bad enough."

"We mustn't talk this way," interrupted Artémise Duplantier, "we really mustn't. It doesn't do any good to indulge in self-pity and we've both had a bigger dose than is healthy for us." She laughed as though she'd cleared one hurdle and was gathering herself for another.

When they came to her gate they turned into the quiet garden and sat down on a bench near the fence.

Marilisse and Popo remained kneeling

until the solemn chords of the Tantum
Ergo died away. She had always been
excessively devout and now looked upon it
as a minor miracle that she should have,
after all, come in sight of the *reposoir* in
time to receive the holy blessing. As she
walked home beside Popo she tried to
make conversation, but he was too surly
and distrait so she gave it up. His ill-
fitting alpaca frock coat and wrinkled
white linen trousers were such a contrast
to the dandyism of his youth, when he had
thought he was in love with her. It was
strange how much he had changed from
those days when she heard vague tales
about suppers to chorus girls and opera
singers in private rooms at Antoine's.
These feats always made her regard him
as a very dissolute young man. Her
father heard wild tales too—nothing is
secret in New Orleans, a peccadillo com-

mitted in Canal Street is a crime in Carrollton a few hours later—but Colonel
Duplantier was a very distinguished old
gentleman, so it was impossible to forbid
his son the house.

When Jacques Labatut came from
Paris with a letter to Tante Sylphide
from his mother, her old school friend,
Marilisse welcomed his visits. He was so
delightful and charming. How different
the two men were! When Jacques discussed the opera, he talked about the
music, but with Popo, it was only the pul-
chritude of the chorus that interested him.
She was relieved when his calls ceased
altogether, and she heard later that he had
returned to the easy society of the stage
ladies who made him feel like a devil of
a fellow in exchange for his suppers and
jewelry. His rake's progress proceeded
apace until he was taken ill—some mys-

terious malady, no one would tell her
what—and he went abroad for treatment.
After his father died there was a great
buzz of talk about the extent of Popo's
large patrimony. Elaborate matrimonial
traps were set to catch him but he es-
caped them all. After the funeral of
Colonel Duplantier Popo had gone right
back to his plantation in Pointe Coupée.
The mystery was solved six months later
when he married Artémise Arceneaux, a
girl from the parishes. Then the old Duplantier house on Esplanade Avenue was
refurnished and Popo moved in with his
bride. When Marilisse first saw her, she
said she was too good for him and now,
as she walked by this heavy slouching
figure and knew the morose, irritable man
he had become, she had no reason for
changing her mind. She wondered if his
illness had anything to do with his sudden

tempers and as sudden spells of abysmal
silence. She would try to talk to him
again. What would people say if they
stalked along with never a word between
them?

"Popo," she began pleasantly, "can't
Arté and Doudouce go across the lake
for a few weeks? I'm going to Pass
Christian and I want them to go too."

"Not for a minute," he blurted out, "I
couldn't think of leaving. If ever this
state is to be saved from being a little
piece of Africa, we've got to work now.
Great things must happen this summer
if we're to make this a white man's country again."

"There," thought Marilisse, "no matter what anyone tries to talk about, he
always gets back on that subject."

"Can't she come without you, Popo?
She needs a rest."

"Who would keep my house?" he asked angrily. "I don't believe in married women traipsing around to summer hotels without their husbands. If *I* can stay— she must."

Ｅａｒｌｙ in the morning on the day after the *Fête Dieu* Marilisse Labatut hurried across the street; as she stepped up on the neutral ground she stumbled and almost fell. This trifling *contretemps* deepened the worried, strained expression on her face and, when Rozine opened the door at the Duplantiers', she was ready to cry.

"Ain't you sick, Miss Marilisse?" the colored woman asked solicitously. "Don' you wan' me to drip you some coffee? Miss Artémise done finished hern, an she layin' up there restin'."

[30]

Madame Labatut shook her head and started up the stairs. At the second floor she rapped on the door and asked if she might come in.

"Of course, my dear, come right in. I'm crazy to see you," called Artémise in her vibrant mellow contralto. She was still in her huge Victoria bed with its satin-tufted tester. The mosquito bar in long pale folds fell from its sides and was draped back to the broad headboard exposing its complicated carvings.

It was such a sultry, hot morning that she had nothing over her except her long-sleeved, high-necked nightgown that reached down to her toes; its starched respectability did not entirely hide the delicate modeling of her body nor the slender grace of her tapering limbs. Her dark hair fell across her bosom in interesting arabesques, whose sleek, satin sheens gave value to the smooth pallor of her skin.

"I am ashamed that you find me still in bed, *chère,*" Artémise said as Marilisse kissed her, "but I slept hardly at all."

"I wish I could rest when I'm tired, but there is always something for me to do. Is it that you were sick last night, that you did not sleep?"

"No. You know I'm never sick. It was Popo. He was dreadful; fussing and ranting and finding fault. I just can't understand him any more."

"If you ever have," interrupted Marilisse.

"I used to think I did but he's different now; he either sits in one place for hours, sulking like a big, old *wawaron,* or he rages and fights until I'm exhausted. Nothing I do is right. Like a fool, I told him that Madame Olympe charged me fourteen dollars for that hat I had on yes-

terday and I've heard about it all night.
Whew!"

"Well, you're lucky, I'd say. Jacques
never notices my clothes but I don't
mind any more. He ought to be married
to an extravagant wife, then he'd appre-
ciate me. He's been fussing too, but it's
about Elodie. He says she ought to be
away from home awhile. It's always
something to give me trouble."

"Elodie! Where would she go?"

"To the convent. Eden Hall at Torresdale, I think. Jacques says it's such a
lovely place, just outside of Philadelphia,
with lots of trees around it. He's written
for the prospectus."

"That's a splendid idea. Doudouce
must go too," cried Arté eagerly. "Dear
little thing! She's so gay and bright but
she's not getting much around here but
faultfinding. Her father flies into a rage

[33]

whenever he hears her laughing—says she's being raised without an idea of the seriousness of life."

"Well, I'd like laughing better than fretting and that's all Elodie does; she's not a bit like me, for I've made the best of things, but she always wants what she hasn't got. Her complaining makes me so nervous sometimes I get a migraine. But of course I can put up with it—it's Jacques that goes to pieces. Fathers never have any patience anyway." Marilisse sat with her eyes closed and her hands clasped listlessly in her lap. "Will Popo let her go?" she added, her mind reverting to Doudouce.

"No one can tell how he will feel about anything but I shall send her just the same. I really wonder whether he is all right or not." Arté tapped her forehead. "Sometimes he gets so angry and excited

that I'm positively afraid. He shouts
and stamps until I'm sure the neighbors
must hear him and wonder what's going
on. It was three o'clock this morning
before I could get him calmed down.
When he finally went out of the room I
locked the door for fear he'd come back."

"Where did he sleep?" asked Marilisse
in a shocked, scared voice.

"Why, in his own room of course," replied Arté brusquely.

"Arté! you don't have separate rooms,
do you?" Madame Labatut was breathless with surprise, almost horror.

"Of course, I couldn't live if I didn't.
My waking hours are long enough to
spend with Popo. I just couldn't stand
any more of him than that."

"But Father Ambrose! What will he
say if he finds it out? He'll make you do
penance."

"How would he find it out? It's none of his business any way. He's not the one who has to live with Popo."

"But you confess it, don't you?"

"No. I forget it."

Marilisse was so scandalized she was speechless. She had never realized before that Arté's ideas of life were so different from hers. No matter how much discomfort her action entailed on others, she always insisted upon a literal compliance with every rule of conduct that her church laid down, even though she was spiritually guilty of the most arrant egotism. No matter how strong Jacques' inclinations were to do otherwise, he was kept from anything but the most orthodox behavior by the constant lash of his complaining wife's tongue. He felt sorry for her, knew she could never be happy herself nor allow any happiness around her because

of her unfortunate disposition, yet he did
the best he could not to show his growing
displeasure. This constant repression was
telling on him too. His black hair and
moustache were graying and his laugh
was less ready. He realized more and
more that Elodie must be gotten out of
this environment if she was ever to grow
up into a happy woman, and after much
discussion and tears had at last forced
the issue.

While Marilisse was recovering from
the shock of Arté's dereliction her pale
eyes roved around the room; over the gay
hydrangea-strewn wall-paper, the ma-
hogany bureau with its marble slab and
little branching shelves, the swan-necked
rocker, and the sewing table with its silk
bag hanging down between its spool-
turned legs like the pink udder of a cow.
She had not yet made up her mind what

[37]

course she would pursue when her eyes lit on the stuffy *prie-Dieu*. This reminder of a better life seemed to incline her to charity towards Arté's apostasy and she decided to ignore it. After all she came to tell her own troubles, not to listen to others. Now that Doudouce would go to the convent with Elodie, she was sure her child would not be homesick and necessitate the further annoyance of bringing her back, so she settled down to the real cause of her visit.

Arté's face was turned away and her fingers strummed idly on her chest. Marilisse looked at her petulantly. Too much ease, when it was anyone else's, irritated her.

"If you're through worrying about your own affairs," she said acidly, "I'd like to ask you something about mine."

"Why, of course, Marilisse, if there's

[38]

anything I can tell you. I didn't mean to be selfish and take up all your time." Arté sat up on the edge of the bed. "What's troubling you?" she added in a kindly tone of voice.

"It's my eyes," Madame Labatut answered apprehensively. "I've been wondering what's the matter with me. I stumble and nearly fall several times a day. I haven't been able to thread a needle for a month or two, so Catiche had to do all the mending. Today they're worse. My head aches dreadfully and I've come to the conclusion that I must be going blind." Her voice trailed off into a thin whine.

"Nonsense, my poor dear. We'll go right to Doctor Barbe. He can tell us just what to do. Probably all you need is glasses."

"I've told you I will never wear them,

that's certain," came the quick answer.

"Marilisse, do try to be more tolerant and less suspicious. I'm not trying to get you into spectacles for reasons of my own, I'm only trying to help you." She got up and put her strong arms around her friend's shoulders. "Come now, let's don't get cross again. We'll go together to Doctor Barbe's. He's a splendid person and has made some wonderful cures."

Arté went to the wall near the head of the bed and pulled down a brass handle. By an arrangement of linked wires it jangled a bell hung on the end of a spiral spring on the back gallery. Rozine appeared promptly, staggering under an enormous copper tub, and placed it in the middle of the floor. It looked like a giant's hat, broad rimmed and small crowned, lying on its back.

"You take Madame Labatut over to her

house and run back as quick as you can to get my hot water," Arté ordered, and then turning to her friend, she patted her tenderly. "Don't worry, *chère*. Put your hat on and wait for me by your window. I'll be over just as soon as I can dress, and it doesn't take me long, you know."

"All right," agreed Madame Labatut.

"Remember, don't worry," called Arté, as Marilisse went out, "it won't help if it's serious and it's useless if it's not."

"Well, I'll try," came the pettish, fretful voice from the hall, "but I've always had so many troubles. They've found the way now and they come to me every time. I can't expect you to understand how I feel though, for we were raised so differently."

"Poor Marilisse," thought Arté Duplantier to herself as Rozine closed the door. "She never leaves a happy thought behind her. She meant to remind me that I was born and brought up in the parishes and was too healthy to have fine sensibilities. Well—never mind, I don't care. I won't let that make any difference to me. If she's really losing her sight it will be a dreadful thing. Poor Jacques!"

MARILISSE was greatly cheered by her visit to the sympathetic Dr. Barbe, but Arté was secretly perturbed when he refused to give a definite diagnosis. He preferred, he said, to examine her eyes again—after a month's rest and quiet across the lake. So the trunks were all packed and made ready, and the evening before Marilisse was to leave for the Pass, Arté planned a farewell dinner at Milneburg.

[42]

She and Popo stopped by for the
Labatuts at four o'clock, and the two
women in cool, be-flounced dresses and
picturesque floppy straw hats, lush with
gay flowers, walked ahead languidly,
fanning and shading their faces with lace
parasols. Popo carried a fan too—a
latanier. His white suit was already
rumpled and moist with perspiration
across the back, but Jacques Labatut
was immaculate, and the contrast did not
escape Arté's eyes.

It was only a short distance to the
small wooden shack of a station on the
neutral ground at Champs-Élysées and
Chartres. This was the impressive termi-
nus of the five-mile Pontchartrain rail-
road, said to be the first built in the
United States. A quaint antediluvian
engine, known the city over as "Smoky
Mary," stood on the tracks, belching over-

lapping, black clouds from a stack that flared out like a huge funnel at the top.

The steps to the coaches were high and difficult, but flecks of sticky soot floating in the air made every one clamber up hastily. Cinders were plentiful too, and if Milneburg was reached with white clothes unsoiled, it was acknowledged quite a feat.

Popo looked as if he had been there and back a dozen times already.

"How in the name of Heaven does Jacques appear so crisp and spotless? His suits always seem to be just freshly laundered, but my husband's— Ugh! They look as if he had been born in them," Arté said playfully, as Marilisse sat down beside her in the queer little train.

"It's easy for him but it's hard on the wife and the washerwoman," Marilisse began, but frenzied toots drowned out her voice as the engineer started his museum-piece through the outskirts of the city. The tracks led to a primeval swamp and, on a causeway raised above the stagnant water, plunged into a tunnel formed by huge, moss-draped cypress trees, each one towering up from its coterie of jagged knees. Not a breath of air was stirring and the cinders and smoke streamed back over the cars, coming in at the windows on both sides. Laughing and coughing, the two ladies took Jacques' newspaper and spread it over their hats. Soon they emerged from the swamp and, with both bell and whistle going, "Smoky Mary," apparently exhausted, came to rest in the sleepy little village of Milneburg on the shores of Lake Pontchartrain.

As they got out, Arté whispered to Popo, "Remember what I told you. Be careful to make Marilisse take your arm so she won't stumble."

They walked under the old trees towards the shore and passed fishing camps and summer places built out over the lake on stilts that strung the whole coast line like snaggle teeth. Just before they reached the water's edge they turned to the right through impressive, cast iron gates into Boudro's Gardens. At the end of a short avenue of trees stood an old raised cottage, and the *patron* himself hurried out to greet them. He sent a waiter scurrying for little glasses of vermouth and announced that their dinner would be served at five o'clock under the shade of his biggest chinaberry tree.

As they sipped their *apéritif* Arté began to smile. She had saved a lovely bit of gossip to tell them.

"What do you think?" she said gaily, "I had a letter from Melanie Ducros today. She's in Paris and had such an amusing

[46]

adventure. She was out driving in a
fiacre, and noticed a fine victoria along-
side. The men on the box were in livery.
She peered in and saw the very distinguished looking figure of an officer all
covered with more gold lace and decorations than a Carnival king. She thought
he must be a Marshal of France at least,
until she glanced at the lady beside him
and then she almost fell over backward.
It was Madame de Grambois Bonseigneur, looking just like a stuffed plush
sofa. Her clothes were as démodé as
usual, and the same old long black hairs
peppered her chin. . . ."

"*Voyons,*" interrupted Jacques, "that
veille Mardi Gras can't be having an af-
faire with a French officer. The morale
of the army has certainly gone off since I
left Paris, if that's the case. No officers
I ever knew were antiquarians."

[47]

"Of course not. Don't be ridiculous, Jacques. The man with her was old de Grambois Bonseigneur himself."

"What?"

"It's true."

"Why was he dressed up like a *macaque* then?"

"That's what Melanie wanted to know so she told her *cocher* to follow him. His victoria drew up at the *Mairie*—the City Hall. The footman jumped down off the box and took in a card. In a moment he came back and de Grambois walked pompously through the doorway; the *Gardes républicaines* on duty came to attention and saluted. If they had had a cannon she thinks they would have fired twenty-one guns in his honor.

"She didn't wait any longer but found out from some friends where the old picture-postcard was stopping. The next

[48]

morning she went around to the hotel and
looked at the register. There sure
enough, boldly written with many a flour-
ish, was 'Colonel et Madame Ulysse
Marie de Grambois Bonseigneur, U. S.
A.'"

"Good Lord, that's funny!" laughed
Jacques. "He comes by his uniform
rightly enough because he's on the Governor's staff—but that 'U. S. A.'—that's
too much! It might mean United States
Army as well as United States of Amer-
ica. That old gasbag let them choose."

They were all laughing heartily except
Popo. He was very cross.

As soon as Arté could catch her breath
she continued, "That isn't all. Melanie
had just gotten through looking at the
register when there was a stir and the
head *concierge* came backing through the
lobby, almost genuflecting as he waved

along Monsieur de Grambois Bonseigneur, again in his military glory.

"He saw Melanie and she said she felt like running away because she was afraid he was going to insist she kiss his thumb, but instead he compromised on shaking hands pompously.

" 'Ah, Mademoiselle,' he said unctuously, 'what a pity I have to leave the society of one of Louisiana's fairest daughters, but Monsieur *le Maire* and his municipal officers await me. They have done me the honor to tender me a breakfast, after which they will in person escort me over their city, so I must say adieu. Mademoiselle, I kiss your hand.'

"Melanie was ashamed of the attention she attracted, so she rushed out of the door in time to see him drive off in an open barouche loaded with French officials; and because she was sure we wouldn't believe it, she enclosed the piece published in the paper the next morning."

"*Incroyable!*" exploded J a c q u e s. "Those dear, silly Parisians! Their world ends at the gates of Paris. They never travel. They think it would only be a waste of time and would interrupt the most civilized and luxurious existence it is possible to live. *Au fond,* the Parisians are the most arrant provincials. They wouldn't know the difference between a Major-General of the Federal Army and Zozo Barber, that nigger general on Kellogg's staff. If they had seen him over there they would have accepted him as a matter of course. At most they might have said, '*Tiens c'est curieux,* maybe it is they are for night skirmishing—they are not so *visible.*'"

As Marilisse listened she forgot her troubles and the strained look disappeared from her thin face. She was glad everything was so pleasant and gay, and she enjoyed the story immensely.

"Was there any more about poor old de Grambois?" she asked during a lull in the laughter.

"Poor!" thundered Popo. It was like a bomb thrown in the middle of the table. "He's a disgrace. With a fine old name like that. . . ."

"Now come, don't be too hard on him," defended Jacques; "he's *gaga,* if you like, but if he gets any joy out of fooling easy Parisians, what harm does it do? Besides, you must admit it's funny."

"That's not what I'm talking about. It's his willingness to serve on the staff of a thieving Governor like Kellogg, under niggers too—yes sir, that's what I mean. Three nigger major-generals over him, and a de Grambois Bonseigneur, a mere

[52]

colonel subject to their orders. It makes me sick. I could spit on him."

"It's too hot to get so excited," interrupted Jacques. "Here comes the *soupe à la tortue,* and to dine well one must have peace."

"Peace! How can you have peace when you live in a state whose Lieutenant-Governor is a Shreveport nigger boot-black and whose legislature is more than half black? We're ruled by carpet-baggers and niggers—all thieves, every damn one of them. . . ."

"Popo Duplantier, stop your talk. This is too public a place to carry on like that," insisted Marilisse; but he appeared not to hear her as he went right on.

"It's no secret that White Leagues are springing up like mushrooms all over the back parishes and they will be able to stamp this thing out. Pont Breaux and

St. Martinville are already organized, and every ward in New Orleans will have one soon. Before long we'll be able to find out whether this is a white man's state or not."

"Ssh!" commanded Arté as the waiter came back after the dishes.

When he had gone, Popo began again. "Yes, we'll show 'em who's running things soon. Looting the treasury and all that bare-faced stealing will have to stop. We're drilling and getting guns and ammunition," he turned to Jacques and added, "You should be ashamed not to join us."

"Spare me, Popo, spare me. Eat your dinner. You never touched those delicious 'busters,' or the chicken and *cêpes*. You'll hurt old Boudro's feelings. Everything you say about conditions here is true, but you're doing your cause more harm than good. You know you're sworn to secrecy yet you blat all you know everywhere. It would get you in plenty trouble at headquarters if they knew about it. You don't know when to stop— that's what's the matter with you. You kill your cause with over-zealousness."

"Mon Dieu," Arté whispered to Jacques, "you're right. I can't decide which is worse—Popo or the carpet-bag-gers."

"Jacques, eat your *soufflé au rhum;* it's the best I ever had," put in Marilisse, "we should never let a bit of it go back to the kitchen. It will probably make me sick but I like it."

Gradually the conversation settled down in pleasant paths, and by the time coffee, cognac and cigars were brought they were all having a very gay time.

Monsieur Boudro came out to receive

their encomiums on his dinner and to ask what opera singers had been engaged for the coming season.

"We don't know yet," said Jacques Labatut, "but Placide Canonge will get good ones, of that we can be sure."

"*Bon!*" ejaculated the *patron* enthusiastically, "it will distract us from our troubles."

Popo's heavy face lighted up for a moment and Arté feared some other outburst, but he quickly lost all interest in the conversation and puffed his cigar in silence.

When the sun went down swarms of mosquitoes forced them to start home. As Arté and Jacques walked along under overhanging trees behind Marilisse and Popo, their footsteps made no sound in the dust of the road.

"These are my rare moments—they

come so seldom," she said softly. "Now,
at this instant, I feel perfectly at peace.
Absolutely happy." She stopped, threw
back her head and raised her lovely slim
arms towards the deepening sky in a free,
graceful gesture that made her seem im-
possibly tall and ethereal.

Jacques gazed at her spellbound.
"Artémise," he breathed. She was so
beautiful it gave him a reverential feeling,
as though the Greek goddess for whom
she had been named, had taken her place
on earth.

Staccato, choking sounds shattered the
quiet. "Smoky Mary" was getting ready
to start.

"You'd better make haste," called Popo
over his shoulder as he and Marilisse hurried along. "We'll miss the train."

They climbed into the cars, lit now by
kerosene lamps suspended from the ceil-

ing, and watched uneasily the winged halo
of nocturnal bugs flown through the open
windows.

The engine started jerkily and pulled
them from the twilight into the darkened
shadows of the swamp. Halfway through,
"Smoky Mary" coughed spasmodically
and died as the cars rolled to a standstill.
A swelling chorus of bullfrogs, every one
a *basse noble* at least, broke out. These
wawarons were like the bass viol in the big
night orchestra and were overlaid by
myriad crackling sounds of loquacious in-
sects.

When the conductor came around he assured them they'd fix the engine soon but
warned them not to get out as the cotton-
mouthed moccasins had been "pretty
bad."

"No fear," shuddered Marilisse. She
was always just a little bit afraid of some-

thing. She looked out of the window at
the shadows underneath the thick growth
of *latanier,* and imagined she could see all
sorts of repulsive reptiles crawling over
the oozy, spongy ground. Every now
and then a loud splash was plainly heard.
"Huh! another old bull alligator striking
the water with his tail," said the conductor
pleasantly. But it was far from a pleasant sound to his passengers, particularly
to Marilisse.

Armies of mosquitoes came zooming
through the windows; huge, blood-hungry
ones. They settled with leech-like de-
termination and began sinking their wells
with alarming energy. It became every
one's immediate preoccupation to fight
them off, and linen suits and dainty
dresses were goutted with the blood of
battle. Someone suggested putting out
the lamps but the ladies said they had

rather be eaten alive than be in the dark in that dreadful swamp.

"Do smoke," said Arté to Popo and Jacques. "We're exhausted."

The smudge from the cigarettes seemed to discourage a few pests but the conductor stuck his head in the door and shouted, "No smokin'!" Such is bureaucracy everywhere. A rule remains a rule, no matter how inappropriate the enforcement. The windows were closed with a bang, intense, stifling heat being preferable to the mosquitoes, just as "Smoky Mary" recovered from her sulks and jerked to a limping start. When they were finally landed at the station they found that the five-mile journey had been accomplished in fifty-seven minutes.

"Could have walked it in less," laughed Jacques as they bade each other goodnight.

NEW ORLEANS had settled down
to unrelieved heat. The mercury stuck
at ninety-six and all day long people walked the streets in a state of deli-
quescence. They hurried only when they
came to patches of broiling sunlight to
reach more quickly the grateful shade under the broad galleries which extended
over the sidewalks of the Vieux Carré.

In the long evenings people sat on
doorsteps and balconies, waiting for the
Gulf breeze to lessen the tedium of the
trying, hot days. Newspapers were
wrapped around exposed ankles and pal-
metto fans were kept constantly going, in
an effort to foil the swarming, blood-
thirsty mosquitoes that soon drove every
one to bed, where they could take refuge
under thick sleazy mosquito bars which
kept out so much air that it was impossible

[61]

to decide which was the lesser of the two evils—stifling or being bitten.

Marilisse and Elodie were still across the lake and Jacques was leading the usual life of a summer widower in New Orleans. The week ends he spent with his family, and the rest of his time he gave to his activities as a cotton factor, a business which at this season and in this year was almost somnolescent. Occasionally he dined at the Boston Club, or the Cercle d'Élite where only French was spoken, the rest of the time he went to the Duplantiers'.

It was the custom among well-bred families to dine at five o'clock but Jacques never arrived, no matter how early, that he did not find Arté cool, fresh and lovely, waiting for him in the dim, double-parlors whose shutters had been closed all day to keep out the heat.

A week ago he and Popo had come in

tired and were talking over the news of the day, when a coughing hurdy-gurdy man stopped in front of the house and ground out a mutilated version of *Ton Regard*. As bad as it was, it brought a flood of tender memories to Jacques Labatut—his youth in Paris, the happiest part of his life. Without realizing what he was doing, he began humming in a clear baritone voice, the words of his favorite song.

"Sing out loud," encouraged Arté delightedly, and when the second verse started Jacques' full, vibrant tones filled the rooms.

"Ton regard, mon âme, ton regard."

Popo ran out on the street and gave the hurdy-gurdy man four bits to play it over again and Jacques sang it from beginning to end.

"How lovely your voice must have

been," said Arté thoughtfully, as she looked at Jacques' slender figure leaning against the side of the window. "Why did you never tell us about it?"

"No reason that I remember. I tried to forget it and probably succeeded. It made Marilisse nervous to play for me and disturbed her when I tried to play for myself."

He idly watched the organ grinder counting his unexpected windfall as he trundled his perambulant piano away, and he was pleased when Arté insisted that she could learn his accompaniments if she had the music; so he promised to find all his old songs and bring them to her the next day.

The following morning had been spent in fruitless search but at last he found them in the attic, dog-eared and torn, scattered over broken chairs and Elodie's

outgrown crib and the rest of her baby
paraphernalia. He resented its having
been thrown aside so carelessly, as though
part of himself had been ruthlessly and
needlessly hurt. Slowly and tenderly he
smoothed out the rumpled sheets and
gathering them up, carried them across the
street to Arté.

"What fun," she had cried enthusiastically.

Not long afterward it was mended and
arranged in a neat pile on top of the
square, rosewood piano that stood across
the corner of the back parlor, close to the
crowded *étagère* with its bisque figures,
glass globes and dainty shell boxes.

Every evening after that, Arté played
for him and he sang—sang back the memory of his care-free youth and gaiety. He
came to look forward to these hours with
ever increasing pleasure and eagerness.

Arté never tired of hearing and rehearing his favorite songs. In time he grew to regret the days he spent across the lake.

One afternoon after he had just come into the Duplantier parlor, Doudouce hurried in excitedly, saying, "Quick! quick! *maman,* ten cents." She had heard the faint chiming of a triangle heralding the approach of the spry old Frenchman who sold cakes through the streets from a box carried on his back. It bore the words "SOUPIR ET OUBLI" in large, black letters—a poetic suggestion of the brittle lightness of his wares.

When Jacques, over Arté's protest, had given her the money, he said, "I'm so glad you decided to send her to the convent. It will be so much less lonely for Elodie. I'll bring you their prospectus tomorrow. Sister Agatha, from our Ursulines, is going to Torresdale in September and will take the children. I'm sorry they can't go before."

"That's soon enough, Jacques. I dread it, but it's best for them both." She looked at the Empire clock, a small Greek temple with its protecting dome of glass, which stood on one of the twin, white marble mantels—it was after five.

"Popo's awfully late. I'm afraid Rozine's dinner will be spoiled."

As if answering to his name, the front door opened and Popo came in. He made no apology for his lateness but began to talk rapidly as they went into the dining room.

"I passed all the ebony aristocracy on the way home," he said. "It made me froth. First I saw Percy Bysshe Shelley Pinchback, or rather *'Petit Bâtard Singe Pinchback,'* as Doctor Durel christened him in the *Carillon.*"

[67]

"No use wasting time calling him names," Arté spoke up reprovingly. "He was a shrewd enough nigger to impeach Warmoth and step in as Governor of Louisiana, even if it was only for a little while."

Duplantier waited for her to finish with a suspended expression on his face, then went right on talking to Jacques as though nothing had interrupted his train of thought.

"He was walking with our *fine* state senator, that mulatto Ingraham, and they stopped to talk with one of those carpet-baggers' bodyguards, the Metropolitan Police. I bet they're hatching out a plot for some new devilment. Did you see how much it cost to support those black and white thugs? The *Picayune* published the figures?"

"Yes, eight hundred thousand dollars a

year," Jacques said. "And for only eleven
hundred men too."

"I wouldn't mind so much if it wasn't
our tax money that's paying them. It's
making us support their bodyguards organized for the sole purpose of keeping us
under their heels. The nigger men are
bad enough but the wenches are worse.
That Françoèse Antoine, the Lieutenant-
Governor's wife, was in the new confec-
tionery store under the St. Louis hotel,
eating *babas au rhum* with a white man.
Bah! an ex-*marchande* of *calas*—her two
hundred and fifteen pounds of fat laced
up in a corset until she looked about to
burst."

"Please lower your voice, Popo," interrupted Arté. "You set such a wretched
example for Doudouce. I had to punish
her today for spitting on the steps of
Antoine's house on her way to school.

That's too ill-bred. I couldn't let it pass."

"I can't blame her, Arté. Young birds twitter as the old ones sing."

"Speak for yourself, Popo. I'm no old bird and I don't 'sing' in any such undignified way. As for your own manners, you may do as you please. . . ."

Jacques made an effort to pour oil on waters that were getting very troubled. "Françoèse isn't as dumb as she looks," he said. "When their last baby was born, Antoine asked if she didn't think it strange it was such a very light *café-au-lait*. 'No, you poor fool,' she answered without hesitation, 'haven't you ever seen a black hen lay a white egg?' They say that Antoine was perfectly satisfied by this analogy from natural history."

Arté laughed easily. "I should be shocked if I were a perfect lady, so just to pretend I am and having finished my dinner, I'll leave you to your cigars and wait for you in the salon."

"Can't we come too?" urged Jacques, getting up from the table. "You never mind our smoking in your parlor."

"No. Don't go," Popo ordered peremptorily, "I want to talk to you."

A queer glint had come into Duplantier's eyes. Jacques saw it, hesitated a moment then sat down with rather bad grace and poured himself out a small glass of cognac. He was afraid it was just a continuation of Popo's boring tirade but was not long left in suspense.

"You remember what happened when two niggers asked for sodas at McCloskey's?"

"You mean when they were kicked out?"

"Yes. Well, the carpet-baggers have used it to get votes. They are telling all the niggers that if they cast the Republican ballot President Grant will see to it that they can go wherever a white man does, even if he has to send Federal soldiers to do it."

"What of that?" interrupted Jacques, who had gotten thoroughly angry. "I thought you had something special to say to me."

"I'm coming to that now. All this palaver has gone to the niggers' heads, and last night some black militiamen broke into a saloon where the barkeep had refused to serve them. They beat him up and stole his liquor. The report is going around now that they're making preparations for a nigger Independence Day tomorrow. Durel gave me an advance copy of *Le Carillon*. It's bad enough, too."

Saying this, Popo pulled the small newspaper out of his pocket as Arté be-

gan playing over Jacques' songs and, to
this obbligato, he read slowly and pompously:

"The *Picayune* has announced a terrible
massacre of the whites for the Fourth of
July. It states the negroes have resolved
to arm themselves and to mob every pro-
prietor who refused to serve them drinks.
After they murder the white men who fall
into their hands, they will complete their
orgy, not by assassinating the white
women but by using them to put into prac-
tice their beloved theory of equality . . . ,
social! So American Independence Day
will be celebrated on one hand by the murder *en masse* of all white procreators and,
on the other, by the wholesale manufac-
ture of little mulattoes—that inferior race
that is much less useful to society than
would be the adulterous offspring of a
carp and a rabbit.

"Therefore, Louisiana men, timid or
brave, you will draw your last breath be-

fore six o'clock tonight; and you, Louisiana women, old or young, homely or beautiful, you will not be killed, but they will operate in such a way that about the fourth of April, 1875, you will give to our dear Louisiana innumerable proofs of your fecundity! Ouf!!

"Therefore, attention, Louisianians! It may be that the *Picayune* is wrongly informed; nevertheless, remember that caution, being the mother of safety, your most sacred duty is to be ready for the fight! Arm yourselves; load your revolvers carefully; clean your guns! Don't attack;—but if the negroes kill even one of ours; if the terrible news shall come that the rape of women has been begun! then, no more hesitation: but, with closed ranks, charge the bandits, massacre the guilty, and never silence your guns until your conscience tells you you have earned the thanks of Providence by purifying Louisiana."

"My God!" exclaimed Jacques. "It can't be as bad as that, can it?"

"Well, we're not taking any chances. Kellogg holds all the armories but we've been able to smuggle in some rifles. Companies are drilling secretly in cotton press yards and halls all over the city. If the niggers start anything tomorrow we'll be ready." Popo's hair was dank and his face streamed with perspiration. "I'm going to drill now," he said, getting up stiffly. "I hate to leave Arté alone. Can you stay until I get back?"

"Of course."

When Popo told his wife he had to go out but Jacques would stay until he returned, she looked from one to the other.

"What's all this rigmarole about anyway?" she asked. "It isn't possible, Popo, that you think you've kept any secrets about this business?"

Popo looked as important and mysterious as a Tom Turkey. "You know that old Creole proverb, don't you? *'Zafaire bouqui pas zafaire cabri.'* Nanny goats shouldn't meddle in billy goats' business."

As he closed the front door, Arté burst out in rage, "You don't know how he angers me! A sieve like that to pretend to keep a secret!"

"Don't let it upset you. He's taking the White League business over-seriously because he has nothing else to do. He's like a college freshman who's been initiated into a fraternity."

"I'm sorry I was cross but I'm dreadfully worried. Something's very wrong with his head—of that I'm certain."

"Oh, no, Arté, he's been like that for years."

"Well, maybe you're right. Let's forget it. Don't you want to sing?"

As Jacques' mellow, sympathetic voice floated through the half closed slats of the parlor windows, Madame Dumesnil, the worst gossip in the neighborhood, and her husband were passing in front of the house.

"Huh! Jacques Labatut again," she whispered. "Popo must be a *'couillion,'* as the Cajuns say, or he wouldn't stand for that."

"But, *ma chère,* don't you think she should have some relaxation after living so long with a *daube glacé* like Popo Duplantier?"

Madame Dumesnil eyed her timid husband suspiciously. "So, since when have you had so much admiration for the lady that you defend her so enthusiastically?"

Monsieur held his peace. He had been married eighteen years.

ALTHOUGH the Fourth of July had passed without an outbreak, tempers had been tense all through the summer of 1874. Over-dressed negroes had swaggered through the streets, while others posed on the corners in gaudy uniforms. The state legislature had convened with more colored members than white ones, and their first act had been to establish a bar in the State House where they could obtain all the cigars and liquor they wanted, free of cost. To the white Southerners, the idea that their taxes were being used to pay for the debauches of negroes and carpet-baggers was as painful as salt in an open wound.

White men stood tight-lipped on Canal Street, when the dapper little black Lieutenant-Governor drove by, in top hat and frock coat, lolling back in the rear seat of

[78]

a surrey beside his fat beplumed *griffe* wife, whose children he had legitimized by an act of legislature. No longer were there complaints that Kellogg had stolen the election from McEnery, that his unscrupulous appointees were robbing the state blind, or that the niggers had become too rambunctious. The time for talk had passed. Now the city was honeycombed by secret activities. A portentous feeling was in the air. New Orleans had become a vast powder magazine, ripe to explode.

This was the condition of affairs on the evening of September thirteenth as Jacques left his office and started towards the Duplantiers'. At the corner he ran into Popo and they walked along together.

Marilisse was still across the lake so, as the time drew near for Elodie and Doudouce to go to the convent, Arté had ordered their little black uniforms and had done all their necessary shopping. A pitifully scrawled letter from Marilisse said she didn't want to come home sooner than was necessary and she couldn't see to do much even if she did so, since the little girls were almost the same size and needed just the same things, Arté could buy them just as well as not. "Remember," the letter wound up, "don't put too much lace on Elodie's underclothes. I don't want her to grow up to be vain."

"That's for me," smiled Arté sadly. "Poor Marilisse!"

Jacques was going to the Pass next Friday to bring his family home, and Monday Sister Agatha, with her two excited charges, was to leave for the stone convent at Torresdale. Arté was getting weak in the knees over it as she packed

the two little trunks and stuck hastily
written notes of encouragement into shoes
and pockets and between little white
nighties to surprise and encourage two
homesick children, away for the first time.
If it hadn't been for Popo's strange behavior she never could have brought herself to send Doudouce away. It was really
better when he went off into rages and
stormed about; but now these sudden
slumps into semi-consciousness, these
hours of staring dead ahead, this drooping of his loose under lip! It was disturbing, no matter how Jacques laughed at
her uneasiness.

She was thinking of all this when Popo
and Jacques came in for dinner. It made
her sad but she determined to throw off
her depression and began to babble gaily.
Pure nonsense is a delicious relaxation
and only a very few know its true enliven-

ing effect. To Arté it was like a strong
stimulant and she very soon became suffi-
ciently exhilarated by her own gay laughter to change her whole outlook.

For weeks Popo had gone out every
evening after dinner—"business of the
League," he'd say vaguely—but tonight
he sat quietly smoking his cigar as though
he was resting after a long arduous task.

"Not going out, Popo?"

"No. Everything's ready. We'll find
out where we stand tomorrow. You're
going to the mass meeting in the morning,
aren't you, Jacques?"

"No."

"You should, you know," Arté said
calmly. Her voice had a critical intonation that annoyed him. "It's your duty
as a citizen of New Orleans."

"Well, I'm not going to do it," Jacques
answered sharply. He had had a hot and

trying day at the office. "I sympathize with everything you've been forced to bear under these unspeakable carpet-baggers, but I'm a Frenchman, not a Creole. If anything happened to me in your fight it would only involve your government and mine."

Arté thought she caught an intonation of superiority in his voice, the condescension a native son always feels towards a colonial of his country. In a second her quick Latin temper had possession of her.

"You married a Creole! Your child is a Creole! You make a better living here than you could in your own land, yet you're afraid to help to protect us!"

"Arté!"

"Yes! Afraid! What other reason could you have for not going to that mass meeting and offering your services if there's anything to be done? You say it's because you're a Frenchman—well—when Germany was attacking France four years ago, did you rush to her assistance? No! You stayed right here in New Orleans. That was your country then."

Jacques jumped to his feet, his face red and his eyes blazing. "Stop! Madame," he said in a voice husky with rage. "I permit no one to call me a coward. If you were a man, I'd challenge you, but as you're not, I can only withdraw."

He turned and rushed out of the house, not stopping to take his hat from the console in the hall. As he hurried along the street, unmindful which way he was going, one thing boiled in his brain—Arté had called him a coward! What right had she to hurt him so?

The rhythmic, mechanical movement of his striding gait began to calm his nerves and, finding himself near the Cercle

d'Élite on St. Louis Street, he decided
to drop in and see if a drink would make
him feel any better.

He found the club room sizzling with
talk, little knots of members standing
around, others sitting at tables, all ges-
ticulating excitedly as they spoke in
lowered voices to keep the servants from
hearing what they said.

A group of men at a nearby table
caught sight of Jacques as he came in.
"Labatut," they called, "come over here."

He joined them reluctantly. The one
thing he didn't want was to talk to anybody. He had much rather be alone, but
since he couldn't, he'd be pleasant.

"What are you all conspiring about?"
he said. "You sound like a female semi-
nary with all this whispering." His laugh
was a little strained.

"Sit down, *mon vieux,* and have a

drink," urged young Pidoux, ringing the
mushroom bell on the table. A colored
servant hurried over and took Jacques'
order for an absinthe-anisette.

"We'll tell you why we were whispering. Orders have gone out to all the
Leaguers and to Angell's First Louisiana
Regiment to report to their secret armories immediately after the mass meeting
tomorrow morning and await instructions.
That's enough to excite anybody, isn't it?"

The waiter came back with Jacques'
drink, and every one was silent until he
disappeared behind the bar again.

"Have you got guns enough?" asked
Jacques, wondering what all this mobiliza-
tion would result in.

"Yes. We've managed to smuggle in
a great many rifles and some ammunition,
but some of our boys only have shot guns.
Loaded with slugs they're not bad for

street fighting, but they don't carry far enough."

"But you can't go against Kellogg and his carpet-baggers?" broke in Jacques. "They've got the Federal troops behind them. It would start the war all over again."

"We're not going against the Federals. They have orders to remain neutral as long as we don't do any damage to Government property. So we'll only have Kellogg's nigger militia under Longstreet and the Metropolitan Police to beat, and we've got to do it now. The steamship *Mississippi* has just tied up along the levee today. Her hold is full of guns and ammunition for us, but Kellogg's spies have found it out and he has issued orders to seize them as soon as they are unloaded."

"But good God, men, you can't expect

to fight a pitched battle right in the middle of a city?" exclaimed Jacques. "What about the women and children?"

"It's because of them that we've got to fight. How can we feed our families if every cent we can make is squeezed out of us in taxes which go to line the pockets of the gang in power? If we can't make a living and our property values are destroyed—well—shooting is less painful than starving."

"Besides," cut in another man, "women and children aren't safe here, even if we're not fighting. Mademoiselle Langlois was knocked down and robbed last week on Royal Street while two Metropolitan Policemen looked on and never raised a hand to prevent it. It was in broad daylight too. That doesn't look like safety, does it?"

"No, nor old Bourdonnaye's murder

last week," young Pidoux said sadly. "I was right there and saw it all. The White Leaguers were parading by when Kellogg's thug, Newton, staggered out of the Sazerac saloon and said drunkenly, 'Look at that bunch of ———, there ain't one among 'em that'd dare tech a fly.'

"Bourdonnaye, who happened to be standing beside him, took issue. 'You shouldn't say that,' the old man protested, 'I know every one of these men and none of them are cowards.' Newton didn't give him time to get the words from his mouth before he whipped out a bowie knife and stabbed him in the heart. I tell you nothing is safe as long as we've got Kellogg and his nigger henchmen governing this state. What we've got to do is to run every last one of them out of Louisiana, induct McEnery as Governor, and let white men rule again."

[89]

Pidoux's deep emotion stirred Jacques
as Popo's fulminations had never done.
He read in the serious tense faces around
the table that the days of hounding them,
robbing them, insulting them had passed.
"You're right," he said, lifting his glass.
"Here's to success—our success!"

He got up and as he went out of the
door, someone called to him, "Don't forget the mass meeting tomorrow."

How could he forget it? Arté had made
that impossible. As he walked home,
bareheaded, the cool night breeze bathing
his forehead, he knew she had been right.
He should have joined the League long
ago, and would have, had it not been for
that tiresome Popo with his continual
loose-mouthed invective. It's one thing
to hear a cause seriously discussed and
quite another to hear it incessantly blath-
ered. Arté should have known that his

irritation had clouded his judgment. She had no right to call him a coward. Then suddenly it occurred to him to wonder how anyone would have a concrete reason for knowing whether he was a coward or not. Nothing had arisen to prove his courage. It never occurred to him to go to the Franco-Prussian War because he felt that New Orleans was his home; and now he had given her the impression he wouldn't even fight for that. It did look badly. After all she wasn't so much to blame. He decided to go at once and tell her so. He looked at his watch. It was after twelve o'clock. Too late.

JACQUES breakfasted early after a fitful night's sleep. As he went out of his house he wondered if he could see

Arté, but decided that she would not be up. It was just as well. He'd join the League first and stop by to see her on his way home that afternoon.

Hurrying down his front steps, he started at a brisk walk for his office so he could attend to his mail and reach the mass meeting on time. He found himself eagerly interested and enjoyed the excitement it gave. Posters announcing the meeting were placarded everywhere. Long strips of paper that carried in black fat face type, the words, "MASS MEETING, CLAY MONUMENT, 11 O'CLOCK!" were pasted even on the sides of the gutters.

He found his clerk in the office when he got there. "Why so early, George?" he asked.

"Mass meeting, sir, I hoped you'd let me off."

"Certainly," answered Jacques, "going myself. You may close up for the day at half past ten."

But it was sooner than that even, when they went out into the street and joined the crowds of men making their way towards the Clay Monument.

AFTER Popo had left that morning Arté began to worry about hurting Jacques' feelings. She hadn't slept very well for thinking about it. Maybe she had gone too far. Men are such silly fanatics about what they call their honor. Of course he just had to be told. It was unthinkable that he wouldn't even go to the mass meeting. Ordinary curiosity would have been enough for her, if she had been a man, let alone the necessity for action

[93]

that even a bewildered brain like Popo's realized. Dear old Jacques! He'd had a wearying time with all of Marilisse's constant nagging and Popo's perpetual tirades, but even that shouldn't make him willing to let other men fight for him, and that's the very thing he was doing. After all though, there was no excuse for hurting his feelings by calling him a coward. What if he never came back? If their friendship was over? How much she would miss him! No one else would put up with Popo's behavior and no one else be so patient with her moods. Without him the world stretched ahead as a dreary, lonesome, boring road, with nothing to relieve its day-by-day drabness. After all, Jacques might have some definite reason for not joining the League. He might know something about it that she had not heard. And besides, lots of brave, hon-

orable men didn't fight in the war of the
Confederacy, because they had principles
which forbade the bearing of arms.

Hastily taking her decision she resolved to go to Jacques' office and to tell
him how meddling and foolish she thought
she had been to try to force her opinions
on him. She would tell him he had a
right to be angry and that she had come
to apologize.

She dressed hurriedly but with her
usual care, running over in her mind the
affairs of the night before. When she
had put on her hat and stood with her
hand on the knob of the front door she
remembered she had told Rozine nothing
about going out, so she called to her and
left strict orders that Doudouce was not
to leave the house until she got back. She
walked up little used streets to avoid seeing any people she knew. After all it

wasn't a day for her to be out. Crossing
Canal Street, she looked towards the river
and saw a crowd collecting around Clay's
statue. Little groups of men were hurrying towards it from every direction,
leaving the other streets practically deserted. She passed no one on her way
to the building in which Jacques Labatut
had his office. Entering the dark hall-
way, she climbed the flight of stairs that
led to the floor above. She felt nervous
and ill at ease. Ladies didn't call at gentlemen's offices, but then ladies didn't in-
sult gentlemen either, she thought regret-
fully. With a smile at the realization of
the dreadful gossip that would ensue if
anyone caught her here, she turned the
knob of his office door. It was locked.
She knocked and knocked again. There
was no answer. No one was there. This
was the one eventuality she was not pre-

pared for. Maybe Jacques had gone across the lake to get out of all this annoying business. With this thought explaining his absence, she hurried downstairs and out of the building. At the corner she passed a gentleman walking rapidly up the street. He stopped and came back to her.

"I have never had the pleasure of meeting you, Madame Duplantier, but I know your husband, so please forgive my interference. You really shouldn't be on the streets today. It's quite possible there may be trouble and I beg of you to go home as quickly as you can and stay there. I would gladly accompany you but I must get to Clay's statue at once. *Au revoir.*"

He was gone before Arté could do more than thank him graciously. It would only complicate matters if anything happened to her after Popo's orders not to put her nose out of her door, so she made as much haste as she could.

Rozine was watching from the window. "Bress Jesus, Miss Arté," she said as she opened the door, her voice trembling with fright. "I done got de big eye watchin' fo' you. Monsieur Jacques done been to he house fo' dat gun an pistol what was hid in Miss Marilisse baid. Catiche was plenny scairt. She set awhile 'cause she was wool-gathered, an den she went home. She ain't no mo den got acrost de banquette when Miss Marilisse an Miss Elodie druv up. Dey wuz each annuder cryin' an ast fo' you, but Catiche tol' em you wuz gone."

Arté hurried over to see Marilisse and found her weeping, with Elodie and Catiche trying to get her undressed and in bed.

[98]

"For Heaven's sake, why didn't you wait for Jacques? He was going over to get you on Friday."

"Because it was getting on my nerves at the Pass, and besides Madame Dumesnil was coming home with her husband today and she said I ought to be here. I thought something might be the matter with Jacques, but of course there wasn't. No one ever has to suffer but me, and since my eyes are worse, every one leaves me in one place until I could scream. What's the use of moving when you can't see anything, they think, but wait till they get *my* trouble, then they'll know what it is."

Arté smoothed out all the chaos and got some hot coffee and brioche for Marilisse and sent Elodie scurrying across the street to stay with Doudouce while her mother rested quietly. Cautioning Catiche not to make a sound for fear of disturbing Madame Labatut, Arté went back home. She was just beginning to realize how broken her night's rest had been and how very tired she really was.

Everything was strangely still; the mule-drawn street cars had ceased to pass, there were no carriages, the sidewalks were deserted.

WHEN Jacques reached Clay's monument, he found a crowd of men milling around. Before very long the street was dense with at least five thousand citizens, many of them the most substantial and respected men of the town. There was not a negro to be seen. At eleven o'clock sharp there was a commotion on the gallery of the Crescent Billiard

[100]

Hall on the corner across from the statue,
as a few gentlemen came out through the
tall French windows and advanced to the
railing. The dense crowd in the street
surged towards them.

The tenseness of the scene, of all this
massed humanity pressing him on every
side, their oneness of purpose, dissolved
Jacques' consciousness of individuality
and he felt himself a part of a giant
weapon ready to be fired, waiting only
the leader's aim and his finger on the
trigger.

Judge Marr on the balcony held up his
hand and a hush fell on the great throng
as he proposed Michel Musson as pre-
siding officer. A roar of acclaim followed.
When it had died down the Judge asked
permission to speak. Quietly and ear-
nestly he recited the wrongs that had been
heaped upon the white native Louisi-

anians. At the end he suggested a remedy.

"McEnery has been overwhelmingly elected Governor of this state, but Kellogg has illegally seized the office. Let this assembly send a committee to wait upon him and demand, in the name of the people of Louisiana, that he abdicate forthwith and permit the legally elected Governor to be instated."

This resolution was passed with another roar and Jacques saw the committee appointed by Musson, and led by Judge Marr, leave the gallery and disappear into the building. Then came a wait. The throng grew restive. Minutes lengthened into an hour and the crowd curdled into small groups which kept breaking up into new combinations, like bacilli under a microscope.

In the buzz of restrained talk around

him, Jacques heard the same question asked and reasked. "Will he? Will he?" and the same answer again and again, "God help him if he don't!"

At one o'clock Judge Marr and his committee reappeared and the crowd crushed towards the Crescent Billiard Hall to hear his message. Dramatically he held up his hand and there was no sound but the breathing of five thousand men.

In a clear tense voice he said, "Kellogg refuses to receive your communication. What do you wish to do?"

Spontaneously came the roar, "Fight! FIGHT!"

It was followed by a rattle of shouts: "Kill him! Kill Kellogg! Ride the rascal out on a rail!"

Judge Marr held up his hand for silence. He spoke again, fiery now, and

John Ellis too. They whipped the passions of their hearers with scorching, searing words, but it was Dr. Beard who gave them an objective.

"Go home," he shouted to the mob. "Arm yourself and prepare to hold your city against Kellogg and his hirelings; to make it an armed camp and never leave it until the last one of them have been driven from its limits. Return to Canal Street at two-thirty today, and you will find an organized body of leaders and men who will tell you what to do."

Quietly the crowd dispersed.

Popo had told Jacques that Leed's Foundry on Foucher and Delord Streets was the secret meeting place of the White Leaguers, recruited from his district under Captain Glynn. Wishing to avoid any Metropolitan Policemen who might search the package he had brought with

him from home, he took a most round-
about way to the plant. When he got
there it seemed deserted, no smoke poured
from its tall chimneys.

As soon as he had knocked on the small
postern cut in the great main gate, it
opened and his friend Pidoux barred the
way.

"Can the captain use another man?"
asked Jacques, "I've brought my rifle."

"I'm sure he can. Come in. You'll
find him in the main foundry."

Jacques crossed the dirty yard and
stopped in the doorway of a huge, sooty-
gray building cluttered up with furnaces,
cranes and moulds. It was alive with
men scurrying purposefully in every direction. Some spaded up sand and
brought out guns and boxes of ammunition which had been hidden there, and
gave them to others to distribute. It was

difficult to distinguish officers from men, as there were no uniforms, but Jacques finally recognized Captain Glynn as one of a group around a small crude cannon, examining it dubiously.

"Captain," he said, walking up to him over in one corner of the vaulted foundry room, "I'd like to join your company. Will you take me?"

"Sure, Labatut, we've got a lot of your friends here. They'll be glad to see you. I'll try to scare you up a gun."

"I've brought my rifle with me."

"Fine! See Sergeant-Major Gautier, he'll tell you what to do."

As he went over to report, he passed some of the men he'd seen at the Cercle d'Élite the night before. "Hurrah for the Frog, that's the way to behave, Frenchy," they called, and Popo looked at him speechless. Jacques grinned, rather pleased. He was enjoying it all.

After a long wait an orderly appeared with a message for the captain. Almost immediately a bugle sounded and the men fell in with a snap and precision that would have been remarkable in a body of untrained civilians were it not that the majority were ex-Confederate soldiers who had had four years of the hardest kind of discipline.

Fifteen cannoneers picked up the small gun's drag ropes and followed the column of infantry past Kersheets' marble yard on Camp Street, where Major Burke had set up his White League commissary. Cups of coffee and sandwiches were spread out on slabs of uncut marble and recumbent tombstones.

The men were not allowed to stop but turned into Poydras Street and marched towards the river. Jacques noticed that

[107]

the side streets were all barricaded at
Canal by street cars turned crosswise.
The great rectangular plates of cast iron,
used to cover the open sewers at the cross-
ings, had been torn up and were being
utilized as armor plates for the cars. Men
with guns were crouching behind them,
and it reminded him of his father's tales
of fighting in the streets of Paris.

As they approached the levee, he saw
the twin smokestacks of river steamboats
cruising up and down. Jacques remembered the regatta scheduled for that afternoon off Carrollton and decided the passengers, taken on for the water sports,
preferred to see a battle instead. The
idea amused him and, as his column
marched along, he laughed to himself.
They took up their position on the ex-
treme right wing of the White League.
As he looked down the street he could

see on Canal a body of at least two hundred and fifty Metropolitan Policemen deployed between the Custom House and the "Old Iron Building," near the river front. Colonel Badger, their chief, was riding up and down behind their lines, and little newsboys ran in and out their ranks, selling the latest editions.

Jacques was in plain view of the armed police, with nothing to hide behind—but the idea did not throw him into a panic. He only felt a certain sense of elation, of excitement. Arté had been wrong. There was a stir among their ranks. Suddenly the ugly noses of three cannons poked forward. Captain Glynn yelled, *"Look out,* men! Get to cover," just as Colonel Badger waved his cap as a signal to fire. The cannon belched and the Metropolitans aimed volley after volley up all the side streets along their front.

Jacques ducked and ran into a door-way.

Glynn moved his men by short dashes to the levee where they took refuge behind bales of cotton and other heavy merchandise that littered it. He advanced his whole line, firing, then dashing ahead to nearer cover to fire again, until they reached the foot of Canal Street.

Jacques' gun got hot in his hand. This game of running and shooting and hiding was getting exciting and he thoroughly enjoyed it. During a lull he peeked behind a pile of bales; all the windows and galleries were full of people. In their eagerness, the good citizens of New Orleans seemed to regard their exposed positions as no more dangerous than if they had been looking at one of the battle panoramas of the Civil War, then so popular. Jacques smiled as he ran for cover more

to the right and found himself near the
little cannon he had seen at the foundry.
The gun crew were cursing with all the
proficiency of steamboat mates.

Captain Glynn ran up. "What's the
matter, men? Why don't you fire?"

"No use. She isn't worth a damn," answered a cannoneer, "but those Metropolitans have a good Gatling and two
Napoleons. Why not let us run over and
take them?"

Glynn glanced quickly up and down
his line and then commanded crisply,
"Pass the word along to charge when I
give the yell."

In a few moments the shrill, terrifying
screech of the Rebel yell echoed up and
down the levee, as men jumped from behind barrels, boxes, bales and lumber piles
and ran towards the Metropolitan Police.
Jacques found himself charging with the

rest and shouting a Gallicized version of
the Confederate battle cry as he ran. He
saw the ranks of the Metropolitans
waver, then break and Colonel Badger
fire his pistol at his own men in a vain
effort to make them fight. Only the gun-
ners stood firm, and their cannons flashed
as fast as they could be served. The man
running just ahead of Jacques slumped
to the ground, and as he swerved to avoid
stepping on him, he recognized Sergeant-
Major Gautier.

The yelling Leaguers drew nearer, the
panic spread to the cannoneers and they
joined in the rout. Lieutenant Guibert
jumped astride one of the deserted guns
and repeated the Rebel yell, while eager
Leaguers grabbed the ropes of all three
cannons and started to drag them back to
the levee on a run.

Bullets were falling like hailstones, as

Jacques followed after the captured guns. The retreating police had stopped at the corner and were firing back, and other Metropolitans, who had taken refuge in the Custom House, were raining lead on Glynn's men. Suddenly Jacques felt a quick blow in his right arm. It dropped useless to his side and his rifle slipped from his fingers. Stopping, he picked it up with his other hand and then ran on until he could throw himself down, panting desperately, behind a friendly cotton bale.

Pidoux came over to him. "That's too bad, Labatut. Let me help you back to a doctor."

"Thanks, I can make it as soon as I can get my breath. It's only my arm."

"You're luckier than Brulard and Gautier and Bozonier. They're all dead! Poor fellows! God! I hope I can get another chance at those damn skunks."

Jacques got up and leaned against the bale. His sleeve and coat were soaked with blood.

"Better let me take you back," offered Pidoux again.

"No, indeed. I'll make it."

The firing had ceased, the Metropolitan Police had disappeared and little newsboys, like well trained retrievers, were scurrying around picking up the rifles abandoned by the fleeing police and carrying them proudly to the Leaguers. Galleries and windows were still crowded with people, as if it were Mardi Gras.

With the exultation and excitement over, Jacques felt like a blown egg. He was unbelievably tired and loss of blood was making him light headed.

He was directed to a store two blocks down on Poydras Street. Pails of blood stained water and bits of bloody cloth littered the floor, but he was glad to see the benevolent face of Dr. Mercier, with his white beard and bald head.

"Well, I'm sorry they got you, Labatut," he said as he helped him onto the counter and deftly slit the bloody sleeve and began sponging off the wound. "It doesn't look bad if we get no infection."

Jacques shut his eyes. It was pleasant to rest after all his exertion.

When the doctor had finished his examination he bandaged the arm carefully. "You're a lucky young man, I'd say, Labatut. That bullet missed the bone and the artery both and went right on through. You'll be weak from loss of blood, that's all. Nothing to a man of your age."

"Thanks, Doctor Mercier, can I go back to the company now?"

"Guess not. You're through. Doctor

Faget has just relieved me so I am going to drive you home. You've got to lay up for a week anyhow."

The jolting of the doctor's two-wheeled chaise over the rough cobbles set his arm to throbbing terribly and he was very tired, but to prove Arté wrong was worth all the dangers he had faced that day.

WHEN Arté reached home after getting Marilisse settled in bed, she sat in the semi-darkness of her cool still room. She regretted her angry words and was wondering vaguely why Jacques had come back for his gun, when a continuing rattle, punctuated by a deeper boom, struck her ears and suddenly her whole body cramped with apprehension. Those were guns, cannons she thought. There must be fighting

[116]

somewhere. Perhaps the mass meeting had finished in a brawl—perhaps—most anything. Popo had been talking constantly of rifles and ammunition, but that they might be put into use had never occurred to her. It had become more a subject of conversation than a possible reality. Yet fighting was going on now. She could hear it. What about Popo? What about Jacques? If he was not in the fracas, why didn't he come and tell her what it was all about? Popo had hinted at so much, maybe some of it was true, after all. One never quite believed anyone who ranted unreasonably. Had Jacques decided to join the League, and was that why he came back to get his gun? She tried to shut the thought out of her brain. What if he were hurt? A man shoved into a fight rarely does it well. Perhaps he'd be killed. She felt a sudden black terror. What if he were dead now! She rushed out of the gate and looked up and down the street. A little band of colored women came scurrying up from the river.

Arté called to them as they drew nearer, "What's the matter?"

They didn't stop. Fear was speeding their bare feet, and the shifting scraping patter continued past Arté without a break.

"Gawd knows, lady, what's goin' on," one threw over her shoulder, "but when white-folks shoots, niggers gwine hide." Then reverting to her *gombo* and the quaint apt proverbs the colored people love, she said, *"Coulevre qui oulé vivre, pa promené dans grand chimain."* (The snake who loves life, better not parade down the main road.)

Arté gripped the bars of her iron gate.

[118]

Her terror was becoming unmanageable.
She felt a scream surge to her throat.
Just then some negro men turned the
corner on a dead run. She stood behind
the large sweet olive as they tore past.
They were bare-headed and coatless, but
Arté recognized the dark blue trousers
of the Metropolitan Police. After that
no one came in sight. The quick firing
and the cannons' heavy booming continued. At last she calmed herself. On
Esplanade Avenue, everything grew still,
but the very absence of life gave it an
atmosphere of apprehension. She decided to go to the Labatuts'; Marilisse
must have heard all the noise and perhaps
she was nervous. She put her hand on
the knob of the gate. The clip-clap of
shod hoofs on cobbles came nearer and
nearer. Arté recognized Dr. Mercier's
old black mare and chaise. She thought

it was going by but it drew up before the Labatuts'. Jerking open the gate she ran across the street. Why should she have that terrible tightening in her throat? Dr. Mercier had stopped there many times before, and it had never made her head swim nor her eyes burn. Why should it now? As she reached the chaise, the doctor was helping a man out. Yes, it was Jacques, but such a weak, white substitute for the angry man who had flung himself out of her house the night before. She could hardly stand. Her knees had lost their stiffening. Jacques' coat was goutted red and his slit sleeve, bloody, too, waggled limply in a ghastly way. Had he lost his arm? The thought failed to alarm her. What if he had? He was still alive and that was all that mattered.

She hardly recognized her own steady

calm voice when she asked, "What's the matter, Jacques?" That wasn't at all what she wanted to say—wasn't at all what she was thinking.

Jacques smiled wanly.

Dr. Mercier helped him across the banquette and up on the steps. "Nothing serious, Madame Duplantier," he said. "Slight loss of blood. In a couple of weeks he will have forgotten all about it. Guess you'll have to send for Madame Labatut. Being in bed with no wife in the house is a dull business."

Jacques started to demur just as Catiche opened the door.

"Madame Labatut came home today, Doctor," Arté began, but Jacques had slumped on a chair in the hall.

Catiche, when she saw the bloody bandage, turned a lavender gray and began to babble incoherent prayers to every saint she had ever heard mentioned. "T'ain' me dat goin' to Miss Marilisse. She done thew enough words at me to-day to make a dictionary."

"Hush!" the doctor said sternly. "I'll cut a hole in your tongue in just another minute. Get some brandy and fix up a bed for your master. Be quick about it, but don't disturb Madame."

Catiche disappeared like a silent shadow.

When Jacques had been gotten to bed the doctor said to Arté, "I'm sorry I have to hurry, but this sort of cannon ball politics overworks the doctors, so I shall have to go. Food and rest and no annoyance."

Arté nodded. "Shall I tell his wife now or in the morning?"

"Better this evening sometime. He shouldn't be left alone. They had a nasty brush with the Metropolitans, but they beat them. He told me on the way home that your husband was all right."

"Thank you, Doctor. I'll stay here until Popo comes."

Dr. Mercier left and Arté sent Catiche over to tell Rozine she'd stay with Madame Labatut, and warned her before she started that the hole in her tongue would be an assured fact if she breathed one word of Monsieur Labatut's wound. The little girls must not be frightened.

"Remember, I'm going to watch you, Catiche," said Madame Duplantier. "Tell Rozine that Elodie can spend the night with Doudouce and have *sirop de batterie* on their bread if they want it. When I clap my hands you come back at once, or I'll hold you for Doctor Mercier tomorrow."

"Quit yo' mortal tormentin', Miss Arté. I ain' never said Monsieur Labatut done got hurted. I ain' persuaded dat was blood in dat coat I done put to soak."

When Catiche got back, Arté sent her to drip some coffee and fix a light supper for Monsieur Labatut, while she went upstairs. As she passed Marilisse's room she listened at the door. Everything was quiet; the even rhythmic breathing of a tired person told her that her task of breaking disagreeable news could be postponed a little, at least until Jacques had had his supper and a peaceful hour or two of rest. She tiptoed to the door of Elodie's room where Jacques was lying white and tired. Her heart was beating wildly. His eyes were closed as she came to the side of his bed, and stood looking down at him tenderly.

"Arté," he smiled, "you're going to say you're sorry, but I'm not."

"Why, Jacques, it's dreadful to see you

wounded when you didn't even want to go to the mass meeting."

She wondered how it was possible to make such words come out of her mouth. She wanted to take his hand and cover it with her tears—tears of regret and of thanksgiving. To see him again, to know he was alive. Suddenly the world was full of music. She laughed happily.

"Don't tell me you enjoyed the fight?"

"I wouldn't have missed it for anything," and then he tried to tell her all his adventures but she put her cool hand over his lips.

He kissed her long slim fingers. The red blood jumped to her cheeks as she drew away from the bed.

"Doctor Mercier was wrong. I'm sure you can be left alone. I'll call Mar . . ."

"For God's sake, Arté, I didn't mean to do that. I'm sorry. Please don't leave

me now. If you do I'll tear this bandage
off. Last night was bad enough. You
owe me something for being so con-
foundedly mean to me. I . . ."

"Let's forget it, Jacques. Here comes
your supper. I'll stay if you'll be quiet
and rest. Doctor Mercier said you must."

He looked at her closely. She was so
strong, so capable. He watched her soft
pliant figure as she brought up a marble-
topped table from the window and placed
it by his bed for Catiche to put his tray
on. There was coffee and an omelette
and the crisp slices of bacon, broiled over
the charcoal furnace, were sizzling hot
with a live coal on every piece. Jacques
had never tasted anything so good and
he never could remember being waited
on that way before. He might have tried
to feed himself—the toast at least he could
have held in his left hand, but he sud-

denly seemed to become utterly helpless, utterly contented.

When he had eaten every crumb and had drunk his last cup of coffee, he suddenly realized how thoughtless he had been.

"What time is it, Arté? You must go home. You've brushed every thought out of my head and I have no idea how late it is."

"That's right. Wait until I've fed you and then . . ." she laughed merrily.

"Don't joke with me. You don't know how much I enjoy having . . ."

"Who's there?" called Marilisse from her door.

"It's I," answered Arté, getting up quickly and going to her.

"Well, what are you and Elodie talking about? I haven't slept for weeks, and now, just as I dose off, someone wakes me. What's that awful smell? It's like medicine. What is it I say?"

Her voice had grown higher and higher, and its strident rasping quality grated on Jacques' ears like a file on iron. He turned his head away.

"Marilisse, Jacques is here. He's been slightly hurt in a fight on Canal Street— the Metropolitan Police and the White League," Arté hurried to say, her breath coming with difficulty and her hands clasped over her bosom.

"Hurt? But you were laughing. I heard you. Why are you laughing if he's hurt?" She was groping through the hall. When she reached the door, her head was bent forward and her eyes were squinted and gimlet-like, striving to see.

"Just a hole through my arm, Marilisse dear," spoke up Jacques. "Arté saw Doctor Mercier drive up and she came over, and she told Catiche just what to do."

"Where's Popo? Is he here?"

"No. He was still fighting when I was hurt." Jacques had gotten up on his elbow and was watching the bent, sick-looking woman in the door. "Come in and sit on my bed and I'll tell you all about the fight."

"Just as usual. Never a word about my troubles. How hard it was for me to come over here by myself—and all because I wanted to save you taking another trip."

"Why, Marilisse, you came with Madame Dumesnil and you said she helped you!" exclaimed Arté involuntarily.

"Of course, but there were lots of things I had to do myself."

"Do come in, Marilisse. Come sit on my bed," urged Jacques. He had gotten very nervous and his arm ached miserably.

But his wife had turned on her heel and was going down the hall with the hesitating step of the blind, her hand on the wall. "No, indeed," she answered, "I can't be made sick by your foolishness. You said you'd never join the League, you didn't believe in Popo's fanaticism, and you really didn't mind the niggers anyway. If Arté and Popo urged you to fight, let them take care of you."

Arté followed her up the hall, "But, *chère,* Jacques had to fight, you know you wanted him to."

"That's all right for you to say. Popo isn't hurt, but here I am, just home, not even my trunks unpacked, and Jacques laid up. No one to do a thing for me. Where's Elodie?"

"She's with Doudouce," answered Arté.

"Well, tell her she must come home. I

can't have her away with only a few days
before she goes to the convent."

"But, Marilisse. . . ."

"Don't argue with me about everything, I'm too tired and sleepy. It must
be late. Jacques, you come in here now.
Elodie will want her own bed."

"But, Marilisse, you can't know what
you're doing. The doctor says Jacques
must be quiet. He must not move."

"Of course he will," Marilisse's voice
was clear and sharp. "I'm a quiet sleeper
—it's better for him to be with me. I'm
not like you, *chère,* I don't like to sleep
alone."

POPO didn't come home all night.
After Arté left the Labatuts', she
sat by her window looking out at the

green, breeze-stirred trees on the neutral
ground, in the center of which at long
intervals, a little street car rumbled up
and down, like a large tin can tied to
a small mule's tail. The light in Marilisse's room burned until almost dawn.
When it was put out the house suddenly
seemed to grow cold and distant. Arté
thought she heard Jacques' voice several
times, but that would have been impossible. "Getting fanciful," she said to
herself guiltily. At last Rozine was in
the kitchen, she could hear her moving
around. Arté went to Popo's room and,
looking down through the shutters, saw
her lighting a fire in the wood stove—with
much paper and kindling and more patience. In a little while her early morning coffee would be brought up and its
pleasant invigorating warmth would cheer
her depressed spirits. How vividly events

were brought back to her by perfumes; sweet olive, coffee, burning leaves, each recalled to her certain joys or poignant sorrows. She went back to her own room and sat down in a rocking chair by the table. As her memory wandered aimlessly over the past, she dozed off from sheer fatigue. She had been asleep some time, for when the slamming of the front door awakened her, she found her coffee at her elbow stone cold. Popo's voice in the hall set her drowsy mind in motion.

"Yes," she answered his repeated calls from the bottom of the stairs, "I'm coming right now. Go into the dining room and tell Rozine to bring your breakfast."

Dashing some water into her face at the washstand, and looking hurriedly at her tired eyes in the mirror, she turned and went down stairs.

When Popo saw her he burst out excitedly, "Well, we got 'em! It's a white man's country again!"

He was red eyed, dirty and disheveled, but gayer than he had been in years. His voice was full of eager interest and he paid no attention to Arté's repeated admonition to eat his food while it was hot. Words didn't come fast enough as he rattled on, telling her about the events of the past twenty-four hours from beginning to end. Finally after gulping down his coffee hurriedly, he pushed his chair back from the table.

"I've saved the best for the last," he laughed. "During the night we sent some men to throw dodgers on the galleries of the State House promising the nigger militia quartered there to spare their lives if they surrendered. Well, they didn't, so we marched on them early this morning. There wasn't a nigger left.

They'd been deserting all night, throwing
their coats and kepis over the rail, so we
couldn't identify them, and sliding down
the posts like big black baboons on a
cocoanut tree. It was worth working
months to get those damn carpet-baggers
and niggers on the run."

"Aren't you awfully tired?" asked
Arté.

"Not a bit. You needn't worry about
me. I didn't get a scratch."

She looked at him vaguely. Worry
about him? Maybe she should have but
it hadn't occurred to her. She felt guilty,
as though she had been caught doing some
dishonorable thing. She realized defi-
nitely how very far away from Popo she
really was; how all the years had grown
a callus of indifference around her and
nothing that he could ever do could pene-
trate it and cause her either joy or sor-

row. There had been a time, she remembered, when he could have made himself very dear to her—but he had failed or hadn't tried. It didn't matter which now, the result was the same.

When he had finished his breakfast and cleaned up somewhat after his night of excitement, Arté insisted he go over to see Jacques. "He's hurt, you know."

"I saw him when he left," he said impersonally. "Too bad he missed all the fun, but anyway I can tell him all about it."

They found Marilisse sitting by the window and Jacques, flushed with fever, tossing about under the misty mosquito bar.

While Popo was talking to Marilisse, Arté went to the side of the bed, draped back the netting and put her hand on Jacques' head. It was hot. He drew her

[136]

cool fingers down over his eyes and then to his lips. She did not start this time when he kissed them, but smiled with her large tender dark eyes.

"Just having breakfast, you two?" she asked gaily. There was a set, determined look on her face, as though she had undertaken a difficult job and would see it through—pleasantly if possible, disagreeably if necessary. Jacques had never seen her so calmly executive. It gave him a peaceful, comfortable feeling. He knew she would take care of everything, him included, and with that thought he was content. For the last few years he had felt he was living on a mental precipice, so close to the edge he could hear the crumbling, crackling under his feet, but now suddenly everything seemed solid, peaceful, arranged.

"Marilisse, you're really not strong

enough to have Jacques breaking up your night's rest," Arté said as she watched Catiche arrange their breakfast trays and do the many thoughtful kind things that only the mothering sweet nature of the colored woman knows how to do.

"I think you're right, but I'll have to stand it until he gets well. I got up once and got some water for him, but I pretended to be asleep the rest of the time. He'd have had me sitting up beside him, if he'd had his way, but it doesn't do to give in too much and I'm not well enough and Doctor Barbe is coming today to see if my eyes have improved. What chance have I to get well? None! No one ever spares me."

"It's too bad. Maybe Doctor Mercier can devise some plan. He's coming in a little while."

Arté didn't say she had written him a

hasty note telling what had happened the evening before and how Jacques, to ward off a scene, had gotten out of bed and staggered weakly to Marilisse's room. She begged Doctor Mercier never to mention the source of his information, and as she heard his chaise stop at the door, she felt suddenly afraid he would drop some hint, for since Marilisse's eyesight had almost gone, her hearing had become so acute that a slight intonation in a voice was enough to arouse undue suspicions and make her ask many and embarrassing questions.

Doctor Mercier hardly spoke to anyone as he came in. His eyes surveyed the room coldly.

"Monsieur Labatut, I didn't leave you here last night."

Jacques opened his mouth to answer, but Marilisse did it for him. "No, Doctor,

I brought my husband in here where I could take care of him."

"You couldn't have gone into the other room?"

"I never sleep so soundly out of my own bed, and I'm not very well, you know." Madame Labatut's voice had taken on an aggrieved tone.

Doctor Mercier paid no attention to her; he was looking critically at his patient. Jacques' eyes were closed and the blue twitching lids and flushed cheeks gave him a very alarming expression.

"Hate to move you, but I won't have this. You'll be better off in the Charity Hospital."

"Charity Hospital?" Marilisse repeated. "I wouldn't think of allowing him to go there."

"He's my patient, Madame, either he goes there, or he's left in this room alone for three or four days at least, with no excitement, no argument and no company." He looked at Popo. The tall, gaunt man was visibly angry. "Madame Duplantier," he continued, "can you come in several times a day, or shall I get one of the Blue Sisters?"

"No need for a Blue Sister. Catiche can do everything for me, Doctor, if Madame Duplantier will look after getting my little daughter off to school and giving a few orders from time to time," Jacques answered hurriedly.

So matters were arranged, and Arté quickly moved all Marilisse's belongings into Elodie's room. Poor Marilisse seemed to take it as a mortal offense that for Jacques' slight wound she was "discommoded" and put out of her accustomed place.

The next day Elodie and Doudouce

said their very tearful and frightened
farewells and went off with sweet-faced
Sister Agatha. After that Marilisse was
quite contented in her new quarters, for
she felt nearer to her child whom she had
alternately loved and nagged to the dis-
traction of both of them.

Jacques gained steadily, but his wife
did not go even to the door of his room
during all the time he was in bed. Arté
moved around quietly and efficiently and
made every one satisfied and comfortable
with the aid of black-faced Catiche. The
greatest difficulty was in keeping Popo
away, for he wanted to tell Jacques all
he had missed of the White League fight.
After the third day, Dr. Mercier permitted him to go in.

"Too bad you didn't see the fun," he
said explosively, never noticing Jacques'
white face. "You left in the thick of it."

"Just a minute, Popo! You know the doctor wouldn't allow me to stay."

"Oh, yes," agreed Popo absentmindedly. "That was it. Well, anyway, Badger sent for reënforcements just before we charged across to take the cannons, but General Longstreet couldn't budge his nigger soldiers out of the State House. They wouldn't move." He laughed mirthlessly.

"Did anything happen to Badger?"

"Yes. Wounded. When he fell, all his men ran away, and the roughs who were watching the battle closed around and wanted to kick him to death, but our Captain Kilpatrick stood astride Badger, sword in one hand and pistol in the other, and dared anyone to touch a hair of his head."

"Damned white that!" exclaimed Jacques, raising himself up on one elbow the better to see Popo's face. "How did it come out?"

"Oh, we got him to the hospital all right. Too good treatment for a carpetbagger, I'd say."

"Did that end the fighting?"

"Yes. The Metropolitans reformed in Jackson Square but surrendered the next morning. We held the city and the whole state and meant to inaugurate McEnery as soon as he came. We had all the police stations and all the guns we needed. Kellogg and Longstreet are still hidden in the Custom House, guarded by United States troops, and they don't dare show their faces even yet."

"Were there many killed?" asked Arté, coming in to relieve Jacques and to try to get Popo out of the room because he had stayed as long as Dr. Mercier allowed.

"Twenty-one, but lots were wounded.

It was a queer fight and soon forgotten
for the next morning when I went home,
there were ladies shopping on Canal
Street." He stopped to catch his breath,
and continued: "On the way a crowd of
us passed the mulatto undertaker's, and
decided to go in to see if he had any
dead Metropolitans. He wouldn't let us
in, so somebody cuffed him out of the
road. In the middle of the back room on
trestles was a great big coffin and in it
Zozo Barber was laid out in a general's
full dress uniform. You should have
heard the laugh that went up. One of
the boys suspected something, so he went
out into the back yard and got a chicken
feather. Walking up to the coffin and
looking down on that big, black buck with
all his gold lace on, he said, 'Well, it's
damned lucky for Zozo that he's dead, for
if he was alive, we'd feel it our duty to

chain him to a post, soak that fine uniform
in kerosene and touch a match to it. That
would be the right kind of bonfire to cele-
brate our victory!'

"Suddenly he tickled the corpse's nose
with a feather. There was a sneeze louder
than Badger's cannon and Zozo jumped
out of the coffin and ran for his life. We
all took a crack at him as he passed. I
caught him full in the seat of his pants,
and I've felt better ever since. It isn't
often you get a chance to kick a general
in full dress uniform."

Arté put her hand on Popo's shoulder
but he shook it off angrily, saying, "Give
me a little while longer, I haven't told
Jacques all of it yet. The worst has just
happened. This morning President Grant
has issued a statement calling us 'in-
surgents' and upholding Kellogg as Governor!"

"What! Do you mean it?"

"Yes. We're to surrender all courts, armories, police stations, guns and everything we captured to General Emory, who has been sent down in command of the Federal forces. We are given five days to disperse."

"So," said Jacques gravely, "our efforts went for nothing."

"I don't believe it," Arté put in thoughtfully, her voice calm and reassuring. "The League has beaten everything in this fight but the Federal troops, so I don't see why we can't win at the next election."

Popo, however, refused to see any hope ahead. His mind was not resilient. The loss of the fruits of their success preyed upon him dreadfully. After awhile he lumbered out of the room.

The days dragged until Jacques was

able to be up. Then the evenings together were resumed, but they lacked all spontaneity and joy.

Popo grew sullen and evil tempered, and for hours would sleep slouching in a chair, with his mouth open and his head lolling on his shoulder, or crouch, staring at nothing, with his lips drawn down as though by a heavy weight. Many evenings would go by without a word from him and but few from Marilisse, who sat with her head bent forward and her hands dropped listlessly in her lap. Dr. Barbe had said she was almost totally blind with no hope of ever getting any better, Jacques told Arté, his eyes full of complete despair.

"Poor Marilisse!" she said sadly, and then she went up to him and held out her hands. "Poor Jacques, too," she added with tears in her voice.

[148]

ONE morning in October, before Arté
was dressed, she stood at her window looking through the trees at the house across
the street. "How alike Jacques and I
are," she thought. "Necessary, yet un-
necessary. Who cares, except for physical
comfort, where we are or what we do?"

Her attention was attracted to Rozine,
who stood chaffering for her weekly sup-
ply of brick dust with Toutou LaBrique,
a half mad old creature of color with
kinky red hair, who made a scant living
pounding up old brickbats all week and
peddling her product on Fridays and Sat-
urdays. Mixed with water it was used by
the servants of careful Creoles to brush
over the bricks in the back yards to keep
them free from the green damp mould
that settles on everything out of the sun
in New Orleans.

[149]

Catiche crossed over to make her purchases too, and stayed to gossip after the *marchande de brique* had gone on.

"Rozine," Madame Duplantier heard her say, "yo' Madame done had her rench yet?"

"Yas, I done brought dat bafftub out a'ready."

"Go git it an empty it in de gutter. I wants to whiff it. Make yo' feets race wid each anudder now, 'cause I ain' got as much time as I has appetite to smell dat baff water."

Arté was much amused.

Rozine ran into the house rather proud that her mistress' perfumed bath, an unheard of luxury, should be the subject of conversation with the servants on the block.

Soon a trickle of water ran along the shallow square depression on the side of the brick walk in the garden and across the banquette to drop finally into the wide open gutter that ran parallel with the edge of the sidewalk.

Catiche leaned over and sniffed it eagerly and was still enjoying her olfactory debauch when Rozine came back.

"Dat sho smell sweet," she said. "I don' see why Madame Dumesnil all time tellin Miss Marilisse nobody but a Basin Street 'ooman put smeller in de baff."

"Dat all she know—dat fat, slab-sided, po white trash. She ain' got as much senses as a *patassa*. An I'm tellin you now, Catiche, you stop yo' cacklin', or I sho smack you right in de mouf. Teeths better to chew wid den to swallow. You watch out. I'm liable to put evvy one of dem in yo' stomach fo' keeps."

"I ain' mean nothin'," hastily insisted Catiche. "I guess she jes evil-minded

[151]

cause her husban' ain' rich like Monsieur Duplantier."

Arté sat down thoughtfully. What right had anyone to blame her if that was all she did? Innocent enough, she argued meditatively, but she was sorry Madame Dumesnil was telling Marilisse such things.

IT was difficult for Louisianians to grasp the fact that the United States Government was not concerned nor interested in making any effort to alleviate their tortures of Reconstruction, so it was with surprise and grumbling disappointment that they learned that President Grant had upheld the cause of the carpet-bag Governor, Kellogg, and had even ordered out the Federal troops to secure him in power. Under these distressing

[152]

conditions there was nothing for New Orleans to do but to endure it as patiently as possible and to prepare secretly for the next election which they hoped would occur after a new President had taken his place in Washington.

Popo brooded constantly over these circumstances, day after day, humped up, gazing at nothing and murmuring incoherently. He attended the first few meetings of the White League held to keep alive their organization as a weapon for their next political struggle but, after a while, seemed to forget all about them and went no more.

The negroes on the streets, emboldened by their Federal backing, had become so unbearably insolent and argumentative that Arté encouraged him to stay at home and would read to him in the garden under the shade of the crêpe-myrtle trees whose

second blooming was making beautiful
the last days of summer. Catiche used to
bring Madame Labatut over and she too
would listen to Arté's soft full voice reading *Émaux et Camées* or *La Dame aux
Caméllias* or intoning in rich cadences the
poems of Alfred de Vigny or the dirge-
like rhythms of Victor Hugo whose revo-
lutionary spirit was thrilling the youth of
his nation.

Soon her two listeners would fall asleep
and then she would drop her book in her
lap and let her soft, dreamy eyes roam
across her garden with its memories. The
last letter from Doudouce would be drawn
out from its hiding-place in her bosom and
read and re-read; the childish, cramped
hand-writing making pictures in her heart
more beautiful to her than those of the
Saints and the Holy Mother in the old
St. Louis Cathedral on Jackson Square.

[154]

She looked at Popo, inert and lumpish.
Our poor little girl, she thought. What a
heritage! Could the peaceful environment of the convent change or overcome
it? She would sit and ponder for hours,
never moving for fear it might disturb
Popo and Marilisse. Jacques always
stopped to get his wife on his way home
from his office and, when he came into the
garden, his eyes would meet Arté's in un-
derstanding too deep for hearts not deso-
lated by trouble to comprehend.

Every evening, when she had finished
her silent dinner, she would guide Popo's
unsteady feet to the Labatuts' door and
after hearing all the news of the day, that
Jacques had taken great pains to collect,
the letters from the little girls at Torresdale were compared, some parts of them
read aloud but other parts skipped over
for fear they would be misunderstood and

criticized too harshly by Marilisse who had become more and more difficult.

After that, Arté would play for Jacques to sing and in the sound of his voice would lose herself, forgetting the world as it was and living, for a song's-length at least, in the world of her own creation where gaiety and laughter and love and buoyant life were everywhere.

When Marilisse was tired she would get up from her chair noiselessly and stand with her hands folded and a consciously patient expression on her face in mute rebellion against any more music. Jacques' voice had always annoyed her and she took pains to let him know she bore it as bravely as only a martyred noble wife could. Arté often wondered why anything so agreeable to others could be so irritating to Marilisse and came to the conclusion that it was because it gave him pleasure and interrupted her constant complainings, thereby depriving her of the continuous sympathy she regarded as her due. At last she made Catiche fill her ears with cotton every evening and after that with this constant, cruel reminder always before him Jacques sang less and less. Had it not been for Arté's encouragement he would have given it up altogether.

"You can't. You mustn't," she almost commanded. "Marilisse hasn't stopped up her ears because *she* is suffering; she's more interested in making *you* suffer. I really don't believe she cares whether you are singing or not. Her own troubles are the only things she gives a hang for. What can we do these long evenings for all the rest of our lives if we have no music? No one cares to come to see us any more, it's too unpleasant. We can't go out anywhere and leave Popo and Marilisse alone—besides, people would talk. Sometimes I think I will go mad. All day. Every day. The same dreadful grind."

"For God's sake, Arté, don't talk like that. I can't bear it. I know how dreary your life has become. There isn't an hour when I'm away that I don't think of you carrying your burdens so bravely and helping me with mine, too."

"I know you do. I didn't mean to complain. I'd try twice as hard if it accomplished anything but it doesn't." Her mouth took a straight, firm line. "Did you see Doctor Mercier as you promised?"

"Yes."

"Tell me quickly. What did he say?"

"Hadn't I better wait?"

"No. They're both asleep." Arté was near tears. "I've been terrified all day.

For the past week Popo has watched me every minute. I don't know what it means. When I know his eyes are on me it takes all the strength out of my body. I couldn't raise a hand against him."

Jacques looked quickly at the flaccid, doughy mass with its limber legs slouching unpleasantly. Swift and menacing anger swept his face. "If I thought—" he began, but choked back the words. "You're tired, Arté, and you're imagining things. Doctor Mercier says it is almost absolutely impossible. It's only the rarest case in the world that gets even temporarily better."

"Thank God!" she said fervently. "As long as he is helpless I can control my loathing and take care of him, but after knowing his true condition and the bad tainted blood that runs in my poor child's

veins, I can only hate and despise him.
I am paying for his nights of revel and
I can't feel one bit sorry for him nor say
one prayer for a recovery I could neither
welcome nor endure."

She thought about it bitterly all the
rest of the evening as they sat waiting
like two slaves for their masters, the sick,
to wake up. Stumbling home that night
with Popo's moist, hot hand on her arm,
she felt the fat, flabby fingers in more
than an ordinary pressure.

"There I go again," she argued to herself. "Jacques is right. I'm imagining
things. Maybe."

After Rozine had helped her get Popo
to bed she went to her own room and
knelt on her *prie-Dieu* for a long time,
her lovely face upturned to the statue of
the Virgin which stood in the center of
her mantelpiece. When she had put out

the gas she went to the window and called, under her breath, to the faint light that glimmered in the house across the street, through the constantly moving leaves of the ginko trees, "Goodnight, Jacques, I'm a wretched quitter to complain. I won't again."

As Marilisse was being led into the garden the next afternoon Arté saw something white and fuzzy sticking out of her ears. "Why the cotton today?" she called, putting her arm around her shoulders and sitting her down in a chair that Catiche had pulled up for her.

Marilisse smiled wearily, took the wads out of her ears and held them in her hand. "I get so tired of the same sounds, the same voices all the time," she said impersonally. "Jacques uses the same words over and over again with the same intonation until I just can't stand it."

"But he isn't here now. It will be hours before he comes. Are you tired of my voice, too?"

"No. Not exactly. I don't mind your voice so much. It's your *créolasse* pronunciation. Those little schools in the back parishes are never careful and it is such a great mistake. They were only meant for Cajuns, anyway."

Arté winced. "Poor dear! I can't blame you after all," she said sympathetically. "I've done my best but it isn't enough. You do deserve a change. Can't I ask Madame Dumesnil to come in for a glass of *bière créole* with us tomorrow, would—"

"No, indeed," Marilisse interrupted acidly. "I'll invite people when I want them. Your tastes are not mine, you know. Besides Madame Dumesnil talks in riddles I don't understand and I can't

[162]

have any company at all these days because I am not able to do the entertaining. You and Jacques have never learned the art of conversation and you sit for hours like dummies and say nothing. He only wants to sing and no one likes that. I *have* to stand it but strangers won't."

Arté took up her book hurriedly. Anything was better than listening to this kind of faultfinding and she was afraid that Marilisse, if allowed to go on, would work herself up into a frenzy. "Shall I read to you?" she asked gently.

"I suppose so," agreed Marilisse. "There is nothing else you can do." Separating the pieces of cotton with her tentative fingers she put them into her ears, pushed them firmly in place and leaned back in her chair with a faint, satisfied smile on her face.

Arté began, tears standing in her eyes and making her reading difficult.

Soon Popo's guttural snores with the lighter accompaniment of Marilisse's regular breathing stopped her and she dropped her hands in her lap, closing her little red book quietly.

Jacques was unusually late; she wondered what was keeping him. She watched the two sleepers hoping he would come before they waked up. These were the only moments she had with him alone. At last she saw him through the iron gate. Her eyes and the warm flush of her cheeks showed how glad she was. He tiptoed across the moss-patched brick walk and hurried to the side of her chair.

"I tried to get away earlier but Placide Canonge came in to see me just as I was leaving," he said taking her hand.

Everything was changed at Jacques'

coming and Arté felt cheerful and happy as she asked him eagerly, "Has he brought a very good troupe this year?"

"He seems tremendously pleased. He's got Chelli and Anna Vercken and they open in Verdi's *Le Trouvère* November fifth."

"What a good choice. It's always popular. I know it will be a great success. I can just see the old Opera House all lit up and seething with pretty débutantes and proud-as-peacock mothers and all those dear simple French Market people streaming up the steep stairs." Arté's eyes danced and her voice sparkled with excitement as she added, "Are all the boxes taken?"

"Almost every one. The last *loge grillée* was sold in my office today." Jacques smiled broadly.

Arté caught her breath. "What do you

mean?" she gasped. "Did you take it?
Don't tease me. It would be too marvellous."

"Of course I took it. I've been trying
to get one for a long time. Negroes can
buy seats anywhere in the house this year
so *les loges grillées* are the only really
comfortable places for us."

"You don't mean that we can go, do
you?" asked Arté, ignoring the news that
colored people would be everywhere. Involuntarily she glanced at Popo and Marilisse. Getting them all the way down to
Bourbon and Toulouse Streets and up the
long trying stairs through the dense
crowd, seemed an insurmountable difficulty.

Jacques' confidence encouraged her.
"Certainly we can. We'll go very early.
It's all arranged. Monsieur Canonge of-
fered to have the doors opened for us half

an hour earlier and then when the opera is over we'll wait until every one goes and we can take our time about getting out. There is absolutely nothing to worry about for I'm sure everything will go off all right. Guillaume and his carriage are engaged to come for us at six-forty-five sharp."

"You're a dear, Jacques. Your plan makes my heart beat like a trip hammer." The color came into her cheeks and she laughed merrily with the sheer joy of it.

Going to the opera! Seeing lights and smiles and happy faces; it was like the promise of a great, sparkling, glittering Christmas tree to a starved, hungry-eyed child who had only glimpsed one, years before, so long ago that the memory of it was dimmed.

Popo stirred uneasily in his chair and Marilisse said quietly, coming out of a

deep sleep, "I want to go home now. I've
heard enough of that foolish reading. I
wish you'd find a happy story."

"How I wish I could! Few of us ever
get one," answered Arté thoughtfully as
Jacques took his wife's arm and started up
the flower-trimmed walk. He smiled back
and Arté waved her hand to him. As he
closed the gate she helped Popo to his
feet.

EVENING after evening passed without a propitious time to talk with Marilisse about going to the opening night.
If she was not in just the right mood
she would immediately say no and,
after once refusing, would never be won
over. She had always confused stubborn-
ness with character and, to her, a change
of decision meant nothing but an acknowl-

edgment of weakness. Arté couldn't believe it really possible that they would go and, as the days slipped by without a favorable chance to speak of it, she became more and more uneasy. She determined to be ready, nevertheless, and got out her *point d'esprit* gown with its cascades of *d'Alençon* lace; the last one Madame Olympe had made for her before she left on her yearly trip to Paris to get new materials and styles for the next season. Rozine had pressed it carefully and hung it up in the large, square armoire in the front hall. Whenever Arté passed it she would always peep in and the soft creaminess of the flounces and the pink and blue ribbons with their fringed ends fluttered in a friendly fashion. The gay colors sent her away cheered as she shut the door quickly for fear the humidity of the early fall would melt its crisp freshness. It seemed years since she had felt so young and gay and unconsciously she patted her shiny hair into more becoming waves around her oval face.

About a week before the opera, with the plans for going still untold, Arté labored across the street, one evening, with Popo lurching along at her side. She was carrying the last issue of *L'Abeille* under her arm and wondered how she could bring the conversation around to Monsieur Canonge. If she could do it, she would have an excuse for reading his interview about the new troupe and it might possibly arouse Marilisse's interest in it. The rest would be easy.

As she steadied Popo's shambling bulk she realized how much more unwieldy he had become. The distance seemed interminable. She was very tired. Her breathing was so labored that she could

hardly reach the Labatuts' steps. When
Jacques opened the door her hold on
Popo relaxed for a minute and he went
sprawling. His uncoördinated legs were
unable to bear his weight. With difficulty
they got him up and into a chair in the
hall and Arté leaned against the wall,
white and breathless. What is the matter
with me? she thought. Am I getting too
weak to bring him this short distance? Am
I going to be sick too? What would happen if I could never go out again? A picture of evening after evening alone with
Popo came up before her and she pressed
her hands against her mouth to stifle a cry
of horror at the prospect. Jacques was
almost distracted and impulsively touched
his lips to her hair as she bent over to
arrange the cushions at Popo's back. Her
eyes were full of hot tears and she seemed
about to break down but when Jacques

[171]

whispered to her that Marilisse was having one of her nervous spells, she steadied herself with great effort and walked into the parlor.

"What an awful noise you make coming up the steps! Is anything wrong?" asked Marilisse angrily.

"I'm sorry, *chère*. It was my fault. Popo fell."

"Of course it's your fault. You insist on bringing him out every night, every night. He doesn't want to come. Let the poor thing stay at home. He needs a rest."

"Oh, Marilisse. How can you say that! He'd miss it terribly."

"Has he said so?" asked Marilisse maliciously.

Jacques turned up the gas and stood watching his wife.

"No," Arté answered. "He doesn't

[172]

have to tell me that sitting all day in one
place is very stupid. But it doesn't matter now. I'm evidently not strong enough
to help him over any more. You and
Jacques will have to do all the visiting,
hereafter."

Marilisse smiled enigmatically, her
thin, tight-skinned face shining in the yellow gas-light like a porcelain goddess, not
wholly cruel nor wholly kind.

She permitted no music that night nor
was there a chance to read Canonge's ar-
ticle, so the Duplantiers started home
early. Jacques insisted upon helping
Arté across the street with Popo, and
Catiche stood on the front steps to report
their progress to Marilisse who seemed
particularly pleased with it.

"Yas mam, he sho do favor a jelly-
fish, wid he laigs a-bendin' forred an back
like he ain' no jints nowhere."

[173]

When Arté went to bed that night she cried herself to sleep.

Next morning Rôzine brought her a note from Jacques with her morning coffee. It was the first one she had ever received from him and her fingers trembled as she opened it.

Poor tired Arté [it read], I am writing the convent at Torresdale today to arrange for Elodie to spend her Christmas holidays there. Hadn't you better have Doudouce stay too? Marilisse had a bad night and seems quite unstrung this morning, so I have sent for Dr. Mercier.

JACQUES

Dear homesick little Doudouce and Elodie! She could almost see their woebegone, tear-stained faces. Christmas in a convent! She knew what that meant, for she had endured so many of them after her mother died. If she could only go and spend it at the convent with them, but that was impossible. For an hour she sat looking at the note dully, then went to her table, opened her little folding desk on the top and wrote in her large bold hand to Mother Anastasia and asked her if Doudouce could spend all the holidays under her care.

That afternoon she read to Popo alone, and Jacques, on his way home from the office, stopped in just long enough to tell her that Dr. Mercier was coming again, and that he would let her know what he thought.

"I've been over twice, but Catiche said . . ."

"Yes. I know," he answered brusquely, and was gone out of the gate.

Arté felt as though her world, pitifully small as it had been, was slipping away from her. She asked so little; the mo-

ment with Jacques, the songs, the silences
—and now she was afraid even these were
gone.

A great desolation swept over her. No
child. No friends. No hope. Only the
lolling figure in the chair opposite, that
was all that was left.

She ate her dinner mechanically, not
noticing Rozine's solicitude, and sat by the
window in the parlor afterwards until
dusk had fallen and the wizened red-
shirted lamp-lighter, carrying his narrow
ladder, had gone his rounds, leaving behind him tiny flickering yellow stars, that
only half illumined the broad avenue.

Dr. Mercier's chaise stood in front
of the Labatuts' house and later, when the
door was opened, she saw him come out
quickly and drive away. Soon Jacques
crossed the street. She hurried to meet
him at the gate.

"What's the matter?" she asked excitedly.

"Nothing as far as the doctor can see. He says she is just highly neurotic, and all he can do is to give her a sedative."

"May I help in any way?"

He shook his head slowly. "No, I'm afraid not. She insists on being alone. Says Catiche can do more for her than anyone else, and wants no one in the house."

Each day of Marilisse's illness Jacques stopped in at Arté's garden on his way home. His face showed the struggle that was going on within him and his eyes, his sleepless nights.

Marilisse was so much calmer the last of the week that she sent for Arté and upbraided her for not coming to see her.

"For three days you haven't been near me," she said sweetly, "but no excuse, I'm better now and Jacques has told me that we are going to the opera tomorrow night."

Arté was speechless.

The pleasant reception was surprise enough, but the complete acquiescence seemed too good to be true.

"Why don't you say something? Don't you want to go?" asked Marilisse, with her head on one side, listening intently.

"Want to go?" Arté cried, taken off her guard. Her voice was vibrant and tense. "Want to go? Better ask a Cajun if he wants *cous cous* and *caillé!*"

Marilisse leaned against her pillows and laughed. A chittering, thin, rasping laugh.

As Jacques had to go out with a very important client of his, Arté spent the evening getting Marilisse's lavender dress ready for the gala event the next night.

[178]

Every few minutes she'd run in to tell some bit of news she'd seen in the papers. Many times she got no response but she was used to that and paid no attention to it.

At last the day came. All the newspapers were full of articles about the Opera, the story of *Le Trouvère* was told in full although every man, woman and child in New Orleans and the adjacent parishes could repeat every word of it backwards. Nowhere was music so keenly appreciated and intimately known and nowhere was excitement so great over an opening night. It meant more than mere opera, it was here that débutantes were launched, social supremacies decided and traditions made.

Arté dressed early and was surprised at her own good looks. It had been so long since she had thought of herself as anything but a sick-nurse that it made her light-headed to see her lovely smiling face in the mirror. Rozine had helped her get Popo into his evening clothes. He had grown almost too fat for them and it had been a struggle to get his high collar and the cloth tops of his shiny patent leather shoes buttoned. When they had finished they led him into the parlor and sat him down in his large armchair on one side of the tiny grate in which Rozine had started a quick blaze to take off the dampness of the early November air. He was mysteriously, unaccountably better, even Jacques must see that, thought Arté as she looked at him and caught his dull, luskish eye appraising her.

Guillaume's carriage, washed and shining, rattled up to the door. It was almost time to start. Arté patted her blue velvet wrap as she laid it across the end of the sofa. How nice it would be to wear it again. Jacques had promised to bring Marilisse over no later than seven o'clock and it was that already. What could be keeping them, she wondered as the minutes strung out alarmingly. The columned clock on the mantelpiece struck half past seven. The doors at the Opera House must have been opened for them nearly an hour ago. Arté was so worried she couldn't leave the window nor take her eyes off the Labatuts' front steps. Something they had not counted on had come up, of that she was certain. With an uncomfortable feeling she glanced at Popo. He looked like a gross statue of Mammon with his eyes half closed and a shadow of a smile twisting his thick lips.

Old Guillaume had gotten tired waiting and, putting his battered top hat on the seat beside him, was taking a nap when

Jacques came out slowly leading Marilisse, with Catiche carrying white gloves,
a fan and a long brocade bag bringing up
the rear. His face was bloodless and
hard. Arté caught her breath in sharply
and suddenly found herself in a towering
rage.

Why should two broken, self-eliminated
people like Popo and Marilisse have such
power to crush all the joy and happiness
out of the world, she thought as she
watched them cross the street. They were
so close now she could have spoken to them
out of the window, but she didn't. She saw
them stop by Guillaume's carriage and
heard Jacques wake him up brusquely
and send him off with a mystified expression on his black face.

Arté's cheeks burned with indignation.
In a moment it all seemed plain to her.
Marilisse had never meant to go. It was

a ruse to disappoint them at the last minute. She determined not to let her know how heart-broken she was and greeted them cheerfully. "You're late, but no wonder. It must have taken some time to attain that effect?" she said banteringly.

Marilisse smiled. "Thank you, *chère,* but all this dressing was of no use, and all your work too. I'm not well enough for any undue excitement so we won't go to the opera tonight. You don't really want to see it anyway, do you? I'm the only one that minds staying at home. It's a terrible deprivation to me but I've had to give up so much I'm used to it. Don't keep me standing any longer, *ma chère,* for we have only a few moments to spend with you and then I must go back to bed." She sighed contentedly.

Jacques took Arté's hand and kissed it. She was trying to be so brave but her lips quivered and he knew her blinding disappointment. He trembled with impotent rage as he arranged Marilisse's chair on the opposite side of the hearth from Popo. As Jacques looked at him closely he realized how much more acutely interested in things going on around him he had become. Arté was right. What did it mean? To hide the tears she could not control Arté bent down to put a lump of coal on the fast disappearing fire and Jacques saw a queer light in Popo's eyes that made him apprehensive. Something must be done. She must never be left with him, alone, again.

Slowly silence settled down on them and, for a while, there was not a sound in the room, then Arté whose nerves were too taut to stand any more strain said with resignation, "Well, if we can't have Placide Canonge's opera we must have our own. Come, Jacques, let's have some songs."

"Not more than one," commanded Marilisse hastily as she put into her ears the cotton she had carried in her hand. "I'm going home then," her voice was shrill and piping, "and I will *never* come back. You're always singing or reading or complaining. We're sick of it. Aren't we, Popo?"

There was an angry grunt from the other side of the fireplace and Arté's face went white with terror. With difficulty she stifled the scream that came to her lips.

Jacques caught her hands and crushed them in his own. "Play!" he said sternly and, as he released her long slim fingers, they rambled over the keys hesitatingly. His favorite song was open before her and she began its melody. With low, even

[185]

voice he sang it to her alone. *"Ton regard, mon âme, ton regard."* When it was finished he gathered up Arté's blue velvet coat lying on the sofa and put it around her trembling shoulders. She looked up wonderingly and his lips met hers.

"I adore you, Arté," he breathed. "Life must be gay and happy somewhere. Will you help me find it?"

He raised her to her feet and they went out of the dim-lit parlor together.

The hall door clicked as it swung shut but did not disturb the heavy, animal-like breathing of the paretic on one side of the flickering fire nor the thin, regular purring of the neurotic blind woman on the other.

(1)

Edward C Caswell